T0121872

THE MYSTERIOUS FLIGHT OF 1144Q

The Steve Mitchell Adventure Series
Volume One

Rick Oates

Order this book online at www.trafford.com
or email orders@trafford.com

Most Trafford titles are also available at major online book retailers.

Printed in the United States of America.

ISBN: 978-1-4669-8000-6 (sc)
ISBN: 978-1-4669-8002-0 (hc)
ISBN: 978-1-4669-8001-3 (e)

Library of Congress Control Number: 2013902124

Trafford rev. 02/11/2013

 www.trafford.com

North America & international
toll-free: 1 888 232 4444 (USA & Canada)
phone: 250 383 6864 ♦ fax: 812 355 4082

Dedicated to my four lovely children Jeff, Julie, Kevin, and Brian for their unfailing love.

Chapter 1

The sign on the front of the one-story office building simply read Mitchell's Executive Thrill Charter. A single telephone could be heard ringing behind a closed office door. It was late afternoon, and the receptionist had already left for the day. Steve contemplated letting the answering service take the call, but his quest to offer exceptional customer service caused him to answer the phone himself. He thought it may be a potential client.

Steve picked up the phone. "Mitchell's Executive Thrill Charter, can I help you?"

"Yes, may I please speak to Steve Mitchell?" the caller asked.

"This is Steve Mitchell."

"Hi, Mr. Mitchell. My name is George McClure of R&D Productions from San Francisco, California. I understand you own a charter service in Saint Paul, Minnesota. Is that right?"

"Yeah, I do. Is there something I can help you with?"

"Well, Mr. Mitchell, I believe you can. My partner and I have purchased a rare African artifact located there in the Minneapolis area, and we're looking for someone to ferry it to our company in San Francisco. Is this something you can do?"

Steve hesitated before answering. It was outside the normal operating scope of his charter service. He dealt with people, not freight. He decided to turn the deal down.

"Well, George, I'm a people charter, and freight isn't a service I offer. Thanks for contacting me anyway."

The man on the other end of the phone persisted. "Mr. Mitchell, you come highly recommended from some of our associates at MinnTown Advertisers. You remember them, don't you? Just a few months ago, you treated them to a ski trip to Lake Tahoe."

"Yes, I remember them, and I'll have to thank them for their recommendation. Maybe I can recommend someone to you. Hold on a minute. Let me look in my Rolodex."

Steve placed the phone on his shoulder and cocked his head to hold it in place. He continued fumbling with the Rolodex. It was old, and the more he turned the knob, the more cards fell from the holder onto his desk. He continued to thumb through the cards, looking for someone to recommend.

George interrupted Steve's search. "Mr. Mitchell, or can I call you Steve?"

"Yeah, you can call me Steve."

"Steve, you see, we're extremely interested in this historical piece getting here safely. We've made a big investment in this and want only the best pilot to deliver it. We've done our research of the local pilots around Minneapolis, and your name was always at the top of the list. We're willing to pay top dollar. This artifact has sentimental value to us. Would you please reconsider?"

"Hold on a minute, I'm still looking," Steve said. He didn't pay too much attention to George's request to reconsider.

"Steve, maybe you didn't hear me. We're willing to pay a handsome price for this job!"

Steve half-heartedly responded. "How much?"

"How does $75,000 in cash sound?"

The phone was silent for a moment while Steve contemplated what the man had said. The first thing that crossed his mind was drug running. He wanted no part of that.

Finally, after a long pause, George spoke up again. "Steve, just so it's clear, yes, I did say $75,000 in cash. I can assure you, it's a totally legit proposition. I told you the piece has sentimental value to us. Our business is doing well, and we'll settle for only the best. Simply put, you're the best, and we're willing to pay you for that. So what do you think?"

Steve was still a little dumbfounded. "Hmmm, $75,000 for a trip to California? That's a lot of money for what seems to be a simple job. I just don't know."

George chuckled as he answered. "I know. Crazy, huh? But that's us Californians. We make a lot, and we spend a lot. I can have the money delivered to you tomorrow if you like. How about it?"

Steve answered, "Can you hold on a minute?"

"Sure," George responded.

Steve placed the phone on hold. He got up from his desk and moved to the office window. He watched a sparrow outside wrestle a worm from the ground as he pondered his own struggle. He had a lot of questions as to why a stranger would pay him so much for transporting a piece of artwork. He wondered if this guy was for real or it was something illegal.

Maybe it was a hoax. Steve was unsure on how to handle this. Finally, he decided to accept the offer at face value. If it was a hoax, oh well. If it was illegal, he could always back away. But if it was true, well, that was too much money to pass up for such a simple flight!

Steve picked up the phone, pressed the button for line one, and told George, "Okay, you've got yourself a pilot."

"Great, Steve! We'll set everything up and have a courier deliver the money and instructions to you by noon tomorrow. Oh, one more thing. Do you think you can leave this coming weekend?"

"Well, Saturday I have a family reunion in Albert Lea that's been planned for a long time. I'm sorry, but I'm not going to miss that," Steve said.

"This Saturday, huh? Hold on a minute," George responded.

Steve could tell George had placed his hand over the telephone mouthpiece by the muffled conversation he heard. The discussion he was having with someone seemed to be a heated one. Steve could hear two men arguing but couldn't make out what they were saying. Finally, George returned to the phone call.

"Okay, Steve. That shouldn't be a problem as long as you can be on your way by Sunday. Is that doable?"

"Yeah, that's doable. I'll leave directly from Albert Lea and head your way first thing Sunday morning."

George instructed, "Okay, I'll send a courier tomorrow. He'll be there at noon. Look over everything, and if you have any questions, you can reach me on my cell phone (916)555-4638. Any questions?"

"Uh, yeah. How big is this thing?"

"No bigger than a passenger," George said confidently.

"Okay. I guess that's it. I'll wait for your courier to show up, take the delivery, give him a receipt, and call if I have any other questions at that time. So I guess I will see you Sunday in San Francisco?"

George's voice momentarily turned from being businesslike to cautious. "Don't worry about a receipt. That's fine. We don't require one."

Steve questioned, "But you're giving me $75,000 and a priceless piece of whatever. Aren't you a little concerned about protecting that?"

"Steve, don't worry. We're protected. See you Sunday."

"All right then. See ya."

Steve hung up the phone still questioning the validity of the deal.

*　*　*

The door to the office opened precisely at noon the next day. A man in his early twenties wheeled in a wooden crate banded with steel straps and placed it up against the filing cabinets.

The two-foot-by-two-foot crate was smaller than what Steve expected. It was surrounded top to bottom and side to side with the metal bands. A hefty lock clasped them in place. It was evident no one would be opening the crate except the person who had the key to the lock. The crate showed signs that this wasn't the first time it traveled. The corners were well-worn, and the steel bands were rusted. The African label markings solidified in Steve's mind the crate's originality.

The courier spoke first. "I'm looking for Steve Mitchell."

The long gray overcoat draped on his shoulders hid the jeans and flannel shirt he wore. He spoke with a low and gravely voice. A scruffy beard covered his face. His eyes shifted back and forth as he waited for a response.

"I'm Steve Mitchell."

"This is for you," the man said as he slid the two-wheel cart from underneath the crate. "Careful with that now. It's a bit heavy," he told Steve.

The man reached inside his overcoat, pulled out a large envelope, and handed it to Steve. He turned and walked out the door, two-wheeler in tow, without saying a word.

By now, Steve was convinced this wasn't a hoax. He was unsure of what he was getting involved with, but his curiosity wouldn't let him stop.

Stephanie, his receptionist, asked, "What's up?"

Steve was reluctant to tell her the story about his phone conversation regarding the mysterious crate. He didn't want her to worry.

"Oh, nothing. I need to deliver that for a client," Steve told her as he pointed to the crate.

He turned, walked into his office, and shut the door behind him. He sat at his desk and undid the clasp to the large envelope. Out fell fifteen stacks of $100 bills, fifty bills to a stack, and a smaller envelope. Steve was a bit stunned at the sight of $75,000 in cash in the middle of his desk. It was beginning to sink in. This was for real.

He opened the smaller envelope and slid a single sheet of paper out. It contained a typed, numbered list of what to do. No business letterhead, just a single white sheet of paper with instructions printed on it.

It read,

1. You are to use your Cessna 310 for this trip.
2. Fly to Lake Tahoe, California.
3. Arrive at 2:00 p.m. local time.
4. Go to gate 3 and ask for Rich Versetti.
5. Rich will have the instructions for your final leg to San Francisco.

Steve turned the paper over to see if anything else was written on the back side. He found no other markings.

He didn't know what to make of all this now. He sat at his desk with a pile of cash, a simple note of instructions, and all this mystery surrounding an African crate in the other room.

Why did he have to use a particular aircraft? How did they know he had a Cessna 310? It was his fun plane. He used it a couple of times for some charters, but that was only because he was flying to remote locations that only had short grass airstrips.

Steve thought about calling the number George had given him yesterday. He picked up the phone, paused, looked at the cash on his desk, and placed the phone back in its cradle. He decided calling at this time was not a good idea. He had questions all right, but they weren't ones he wanted to ask. The money loomed too big in his eyes for such a simple trip. Granted, flying the 310 would make for a longer flight than he originally thought, but he had $75,000 to do it! *Flying the 310 would be just fine.*

He wrote George's phone number on a piece of scratch paper and slipped it in the middle drawer of his desk. Steve gathered the cash and placed it in his briefcase along with the letter of instructions. He then grabbed a two-wheel cart out of the storage room and left that afternoon without saying much more to Stephanie. He told her he had two stops to make: his Cessna 310 and the bank. As he pulled from the parking lot, he had $75,000 in a briefcase and the crate in his trunk.

*   *   *

It was an early May morning, and the sun was just clearing the horizon to greet the day. Steve was daydreaming as he drove his red convertible BMW to the airport in downtown Saint Paul, Minnesota. Steve enjoyed fast cars, fast planes, and fast women. His muscular six-foot-two body with blond wavy hair and blue eyes made him an attraction at the local clubs, gas stations, grocery stores, and just about anywhere he went. There never was a shortage of beautiful, attractive women at his side. He had a mystic allure that made him irresistible to the single woman as well as the married ones.

Steve lived the life of a typical bachelor. He came and went as he pleased. He answered to no one. At the age of thirty-one, he didn't plan to be single but he was.

There was a time while stationed in Hawaii with the air force that he came close to getting married. Steve's affections were held captive by a Hawaiian transplant from Texas named April Thompson. Her curvaceous figure, flowing dark hair, and sweet disposition instantly attracted his attention. It was not long after their first meeting that Steve found himself completely entrusting his heart, his dreams, and his hopes to her.

They first met in a small beach town named Lahaina on the island of Maui. It was located just on the edge of the Ka'anapali resort strip. The town was almost entirely made up of small souvenir and clothing shops. Steve, on a two-day pass from military duty, stopped to eat at the Paradise Burger Grill located on the ocean side of the main strip. The two-story, open-air restaurant claimed to have the best burgers on the island. The restaurant decor had an island-castaway appeal to it. The picturesque view overlooking the ocean was simply breathtaking.

Steve parked his car two blocks from the restaurant and enjoyed a leisurely stroll past the tourist-trinket shops. It felt good to be out from under the watchful eye of the air force for a couple of days. The five-plus years he had served thus far in the military was an event in Steve's life that shaped his future. However, for the next two days, he wasn't concerned about the future or anything else for that matter. He wanted to enjoy doing what he pleased, when he pleased, and doing it without a military time schedule.

Steve climbed the wooden-and-bamboo stairs to the second floor of the restaurant. He wanted to feel as much of the ocean breeze as possible.

He asked the greeter at the top, "May I please have a table overlooking the water?"

The greeter quickly scooped up a menu and responded, "We just had one of our best tables open up. Follow me please."

Steve, sporting jeans and a T-shirt, settled into a corner table that had a terrific view of the crashing surf. A cool breeze was blowing slightly from the ocean. Rarely was he allowed in public without wearing his military uniform, and the temporary freedom from it allowed him to feel the full effects of the breeze. It felt very relaxing to him.

"Can I get you anything to drink, sir?" the greeter asked.

"Why don't you give me a minute? Thanks anyway," Steve answered.

He was busy looking over the menu choices when he heard a sultry voice.

"Good afternoon, sir. Have you had a chance to decide what you want?"

Steve looked up and saw the most beautiful waitress with the cutest smile he'd ever seen. The name tag on her uniform simply said April. He hesitated to answer because he was so immediately awestruck with her beauty. The breeze was gently brushing her auburn-colored hair over the creamy complexion of her cheeks. Her skin was flawless. Her brown eyes seemed to pierce his ability to think clearly. Steve was captivated by her appearance.

"Uh, uh, no . . . no, I haven't, could you give me a . . . a couple of minutes?" he managed to stammer. Steve's ever-confident demeanor was shaken a bit. April had a natural beauty that was stunning.

"No problem, dear," she replied with a smile. "Just flag me down when you are ready."

April placed the glass of water she was carrying on the table and left with a smirk on her face. She could tell by his startled composure that she had been quite impressionable to him. Her smile continued into the kitchen area.

April returned after a few minutes and asked for his order. Steve chose the cheeseburger house special and an iced tea.

"Great choice. I'll get that right out for you," April said.

She paused shortly to admire his wavy blond hair. She could tell by his chiseled physique that he had to be a military man. His shoulders were broad, and she could envision his muscle-toned chest behind the white T-shirt he wore. He sat upright and had a can-do attitude that was very evident. She wondered what his name was and if he was new to the area.

April had seen a good many people during the two years she was in Hawaii. After graduating from Texas A&M with a degree in business, she and a friend agreed that it was time to take a few months off and enjoy the freedom. They both decided Maui was the perfect place to do that. After a couple of months, her friend became homesick and returned stateside. April only planned to stay a total of six months herself and then return. That was over a year ago, and she hadn't left yet.

April enjoyed being a waitress at the Paradise Burger Grill because it allowed her to meet such a diverse group of people. Her beauty tempted a fair amount of men to initially try to flirt their way into her life. None were successful. However, that soon could change. Steve hadn't tried to flirt, but she found herself wishing he would.

She entered the kitchen and mumbled to herself, "Goodness, girl, all he did was order a burger! Maybe I should do the flirting this time."

She placed the order on the cook's window with a slight smile showing on her face.

April returned with Steve's iced tea. She placed the drink on the table.

"Here ya go, sailor."

"Sailor?" he said excitedly. "What makes you think I'm a sailor?"

"Oh, nothing, just guessing," April replied.

"Well, just to set the record straight, no navy for me. I hang my hat in the air force as a jet jockey," he said jokingly.

April just nodded with raised eyebrows, turned, and went about her work. Steve watched her move throughout the restaurant, attending to the other patrons. He couldn't keep his eyes off her. He could not believe how his emotions were reacting! He certainly was attracted to her. He had to know more about her.

April returned with his meal.

"One house special for a very special air force—jet jockey, was it?" She gave a mischievous smirk.

Her attempt to flirt was evident. She was a little embarrassed over her actions and quickly asked if he cared for any mustard or ketchup.

"No thanks, this will do," he replied.

April turned and walked away before he could see her blushing. She felt a bit uncomfortable with her approach. Normally, she was so much smoother.

After lunch, Steve planned to wander the shops for a little bit and then return that afternoon for a dessert as an excuse to see her again. As he ate his meal, both cast smiles at one another as small gestures of flirting. He finished his lunch and left a $5.00 tip for an $8.79 meal, hoping she would remember him when he returned. As he was leaving, he smiled brightly at April. She smiled sweetly back. Steve left the restaurant that afternoon with April on his mind.

After about an hour, his emotions leaped with excitement to see her in one of the local shops at the freshwater pearl display. He made a point to stop and say hi. She gave a genuine smile as the two of them made eye contact.

"Oh, you remember me, huh?" Steve asked with a little sarcasm.

April replied flirtatiously, "Of course I do. I never forget a handsome face."

Without breaking stride, she held out two necklace selections of freshwater pearls from the counter display and asked, "Which do you like better, the pink or the blue?"

"Definitely the blue," Steve said.

"My choice exactly," she replied as she handed the strands back to the salesperson. "Save those for me, and I'll be back later this week for them."

Turning back to Steve, she said, "Thanks, Mr . . . . uh . . . uh." Gesturing with her hands, she attempted to get Steve to reveal his name.

"Oh, Steve . . . Steve Mitchell," he finally replied.

"Well, thanks, Mr. Steve . . . Steve Mitchell," she responded with a giggle.

She smiled, turned, and walked out the door. She felt confident in her flirtatious approach this time.

Steve followed her with his eyes as she disappeared around the corner. He stepped up to the display April had just left and told the clerk, "I'll take the blue ones, and could you please gift wrap that for me?"

The salesclerk gave a pleasing smile. She sensed what Steve had in mind.

"That's mighty sweet of you, and that'll be $56.89 with tax," the clerk said.

Steve waited for the pearls to be gift wrapped and left. He decided to return to the Paradise Burger Grill with the pearls the next day. He definitely was attracted to April but didn't want to appear overly anxious.

That night, Steve stayed at one of the resorts on the beach. For three hours, he laid in a hammock stretched between two palm trees, enjoying the Hawaiian climate and thinking of April. He was watching the sun set over the water with one leg draped over the edge. He slowly swung the hammock back and forth. He wondered if she would be working tomorrow when he returned to the ocean-side grill. If not, with his military schedule, it was going to be difficult to get back to see her. He was a little upset with himself for not asking for April's telephone number. He knew better. When it came to meeting women, he wasn't a rookie.

April went home that day and didn't think too much more of Steve. Although she enjoyed being around him for such a brief time, she really didn't think she would see him again. A good majority of the customers who came through the restaurant were transient individuals, here today and gone tomorrow. Rarely was there a regular, or at least a regular who April was attracted to.

The next day, Steve returned to the Paradise Burger Grill with his neatly wrapped package of freshwater pearls tucked under his arm. He was anxious as he climbed the stairs to the second story of the restaurant. He wondered if she would be working.

Steve met the restaurant greeter at the top of the stairs and asked, "Hi. Is April working today?"

"She most certainly is. Would you like to sit in her section?"

"That would be nice," Steve replied.

The greeter led Steve through a section filled with camera-laden tourists having lunch and seated him at a corner table in the section where April was serving. Steve watched her as she went about her work. She had not yet glanced at his table. With her hair gently whisking across the softness of her face, her beauty was more evident than he remembered. Her voice seemed to be that of an angel.

April was serving an older couple their lunch when she glanced at the corner table and saw Steve. An immediate, genuine smile came to her face. She wiped her hands on the apron she was wearing and went directly to his table.

"Well, Mr. Steve Mitchell, back so soon?" she said smiling at him.

"Yes, yes, I am. Can't stay away from a good thing."

Steve wanted it to sound like he was referring to the restaurant when actually he was speaking of her. He could tell by her facial expressions that she heard him in the manner he meant it.

He lifted the gift-wrapped pearls from his lap and handed them toward April.

"I hope you're not offended by this. I enjoy giving small gifts to strangers." Steve was trying to make light of the situation. It was a bit of an awkward approach, and he thought a little humor would break the ice.

She accepted the package with a surprised expression.

"For me?" she exclaimed as she sat down across from Steve to carefully open the package. "The blue ones! How very thoughtful of you," she said.

"Oh, it was my pleasure."

April couldn't help but ask, "So, Mr. Mitchell, why did you think you needed to buy me a gift? I don't think you were quite honest when you said you like to do this for strangers."

Steve chuckled and said, "Yeah, I guess you're right. I don't often do this for strangers, just the ones that are beautiful."

"Well, thank you, Mr. Mitchell, or can I call you Steve? And the compliment about beauty works for me."

"Well, the name Steve works for me. By the way, what time do you get off today?"

"At three," she answered. She didn't have to ask why. She could see he was attracted to her and was interested in seeing her more than at the restaurant.

"After work, would you like to go for a walk with me in the park?"

"I would be honored," she stoically said.

"Great! Well, I'll have a piece of coconut pie and an iced tea for now," Steve said with a smile.

April left his table with the box of freshwater pearls tucked under her arm. While at the waitress station, she opened the box and put the necklace on that Steve had just given her. When she returned with his order, he looked at her and winked. "Yep, the blue ones were definitely the right choice." She smiled and went about her work.

He finished his dessert and told April he would be back at three that afternoon. As he descended the bamboo stairs to leave the restaurant, he felt different. There was an excitement in the air.

April spent the rest of her shift as if she was floating on air. Although she was a beautiful woman, it had been a long time since someone as good-looking as Steve had asked her for a date. It was even longer since someone had given her a gift for no special reason. He had certainly impressed her. Very few men had been able to get close enough to do that.

After her shift, the two of them met outside the restaurant and walked to the nearby seaside park. From then on, things were never the same. They walked along the beach, talking about each other's lives. They discussed how each had arrived at the place in life they were in. April was fascinated with Steve being a pilot. She had an appetite for adventure, and his pilot stories fed that hunger.

The two of them talked well past sunset and long into the night. They were sitting beneath a palm tree overlooking the moonlit ocean when both agreed it was getting late and they should go. Before parting, Steve kissed April softly. Even though it was only a single kiss, it seemed so natural and perfect. Both had wanted it to happen.

For the remainder of the year, the two of them spent a lot of time together. They spent many hours simply talking and learning each other's likes and dislikes. The initial flirting each had done with the other had now turned into a steamy romance. They spent time together running on the beach, biking, shopping, and having small talks at the local coffee shop. But their all-time favorite was taking passionate walks on the sandy beach.

Their romance flourished over the next several months. No other woman had ever fully pleased him more. Steve had completely fallen in love with April. He had many romances before, but with April, it was different. He felt a relational comfort with her like no other. He allowed his entire life to be consumed by her.

April too had fallen in love with him. She found him to be fun and adventurous. He loved her in so many ways. The pearls he had given her the day of their first date was just the start. He continued to shower her with jewelry and gifts. Although she told him she loved him, deep down April was not letting go completely. Her love life inside was like a fleeing bird. At any moment, it could be scared into flight, never to return.

Just prior to the Thanksgiving holiday, Steve was convinced April was the woman he wanted to spend the rest of his life with. He thought she was perfect for him. He never had so much fun with anyone else as he did with April. He could not stand to be apart from her. Steve decided it was time to propose marriage.

He had a romantic and fun-filled night planned for the occasion. He had already chosen the most gorgeous diamond ring he could find. He was sure April would like it because during a recent window-shopping date, she had seen the ring in the jeweler's window. She swooned over the ring and how beautiful it was.

It was early on Friday evening when Steve, dressed in a black tuxedo, arrived at April's apartment to pick her up. He had previously told her the date was going to be formal. She didn't know if he would propose, but she had her suspicions and hopes.

April answered the door in a stunning outfit. The sun was setting behind her as she stood in the doorway. The rays of sunshine outlined her slender figure, giving her the appearance of an angel in Steve's eyes. The image of beauty was permanently engraved in Steve's mind.

The designer silk dress she wore gently blew in the island breeze. Around her neck, she wore the blue freshwater pearls Steve had given to her many months earlier. He marveled at how beautiful she was. He was on top of the world that night.

Steve took April for a romantic candlelit dinner. During the meal, they stared at one another with a love neither had experienced before. April looked deep into Steve's eyes. She imagined she could see through to the deepest part of his emotions. There she saw her soul entwined with his. Without a spoken word, she could hear the love Steve had for her. It was in every move, every touch, and in every word. Both were feeling as though it was heaven on earth.

After dinner, for fun, Steve took April to the Paradise Burger Grill for dessert. There they laughed at the silliest things. They were enjoying themselves immensely. As the night progressed, April's hope for an engagement ring faded. The romantic touch they had been experiencing was now replaced with laughter and silliness. She felt that if he was going to propose, he would have done it during the earlier romantic dinner.

Leaving the grill, Steve turned to April and said, "Let's go for a walk in the park. We haven't been there in a long time."

They walked along the sandy seaside beach hand in hand. The surf provided a soothing rhythm that relaxed both of them. April assumed it was just a random walk with no place to go in mind. However, Steve had other ideas. He stopped next to a very special palm tree. It was the same one where he first kissed her many months earlier. April was facing the ocean, watching the moonlight dance on the waves. Each sparkle seemingly kissed the horizon.

Steve dropped to one knee and took April's left hand in his. He pulled the engagement ring from his pocket. He placed it on her finger. As she moved her hand in the moonlight, each point of the diamond shimmered with a radiant ray of color and light.

"April, I have given you my heart, and now I want to give you my life. I want to spend the rest of it with you as my wife. Will you marry me?"

The engagement ring glimmered under the light of a full moon while the surf pounded the beach as if applauding the occasion. April paused while trying to hold back the emotions that swept over her. Finally, she answered.

"Yes, Steve, I would be happy to be your wife."

The remainder of the night, they held tight to each other under the moonlight, basking in the glow of a love Steve never knew could be so satisfying. He felt a sense of security by placing his heart in her hands. He had full and complete trust in her that she would guard the emotions of his heart for life. As the night ended, April began having second thoughts.

One month later at 3:00 a.m., the doorbell rang, and the sound of a car door slamming woke Steve from a sound sleep. He heard the car drive off as he pulled himself from bed and stumbled to the door in a state of drowsiness. He opened the door to find a single rose with a card tied to it and a small box.

Puzzled, he bent down and picked up the items. He closed the door with a fear of uncertainty in his heart. He had no idea what he was about to face. His hands trembled as he hastily opened the small box. To his surprise, inside was the engagement ring he had given April. Steve dropped to the couch in a state of bewilderment as he pulled the card from the rose stem. The handwritten card simply said,

Dear Steve,

I am sorry for the hurt you are about to feel, but I would rather hurt you now and get on with life than hurt you later. I can't live the life of being your wife. I need my space to be free. I am sorry, darling. Have a good life.

Love, April

Steve tried to telephone her, but it just kept ringing without any answer. He quickly dressed, jumped into his car, and drove wildly to her apartment only to find it as empty as his heart was feeling. Steve never saw April again. She simply disappeared from his life without any further explanation. Steve felt an almost incapacitating devastation.

He spent the next couple of months being the best pilot he could be. He would fly the maximum amount of hours he was allowed. He felt free up in the sky. In the air, he was alone with only his aircraft to control in a wide-open sky. "Life goes on" was his motto.

However, deep down, he was hurt much more than he wanted to admit.

Three months later, on a particularly quiet evening, Steve was feeling especially lonely and in a state of despair. His emotions were heavily tearing at his heart. He had seen April's engagement ring one too many times on the corner of his bedroom nightstand where he had left it. He knew he had to do something to bring closure to his romance with her. Without hesitation, he grabbed the now-dried rose, the ring, and the card and jumped in his car and headed for the ocean-cliff overlook near his apartment. He didn't care that it was 1:00 a.m. He knew what he had to do.

When he arrived, he walked to the rocky edge and made one final glance at the three items he held in his hands. Their memories were forever etched in his mind. He had read the card so many times, his tears had blurred the printing of the words.

Over the roar of the pounding surf, Steve yelled, "I will always love you, April."

He then tossed the dried rose, the card, and the ring as far into the sea as he could. He watched them disappear into the watery darkness. He was done with her for good. He had to move on. He vowed from that day forward, no woman would ever have that much control of his heart again.

He heard later that April had run off with a shipping merchant to travel the world. He guessed she was pursuing adventure. He wished he could have talked to her. He just wanted to ask why. Maybe he could have convinced her to change her mind or maybe not. Now all he had were her memories and unfulfilled dreams of a lost love.

He never again visited the Paradise Burger Grill after April left, and he had no plans of ever going there again. He wanted to keep the memory of how they met as a good memory in his past. He didn't want to return and be haunted forever by not seeing her there.

Six months later, Steve was granted an honorable discharge from the air force and moved from Hawaii back to the mainland. He left behind the bad experience, but he held tightly to the good memories of loving April.

Steve remembered the long moonlit walks on a gentle sandy beach. He remembered the palm tree where they kissed for the first time. It was the same spot where he had proposed to April. They were bittersweet memories. As hard as he tried to forget them, they were not diminishing from his thought pattern.

After his discharge from the air force, Steve moved from Hawaii to Saint Paul, Minnesota, and lived the typical bachelor life. With the money he had saved while in the service, he decided to start his own business. His father was hoping Steve would return to the family crop-dusting business, but Steve couldn't fathom going back to work for his family. Even though he loved his parents, he felt he couldn't put up with being told what to do, when to do it, and how to do it! He had enough of that in the military.

He now wanted to live life carefree with no one to answer to but himself. He had his own mark to make in life, and he wanted to do it his way and in style.

Steve came up with an ingenious business plan that sold high-adventure vacations to top business executives. His business model included an air-charter service as well as implementing the adventure once he had arrived with his guests at a predetermined destination. He presold these adventure-vacation packages to executives for thousands of dollars. The thrill-seeking executives would not be disappointed. The trips were all-inclusive, including chartered air travel, food, lodging, and entertainment. Steve's excursions were always first-class productions.

Collecting a deposit in advance from several executives and a family loan provided Steve the cash flow to get started as Mitchell's Executive Thrill Charter. After four years, the flying adventures were doing very well. The money collected from his excursions seemed to flow freely right into Steve's pocket. He was fortunate to build his business around top-notch business executives. He knew money would not be an issue with them, and it never was. Many of his clients were repeat customers. Steve made it easy for those companies to entertain their very best clients in style.

Recently, he had chartered four big-name advertising executives from MinnTown Advertisers to Lake Tahoe for a little helicopter-drop skiing. It was late in the season to ski, but some of the higher elevations still had some great opportunities for the brave at heart.

Helicopter-drop skiing consists of jumping from a helicopter into mostly virgin mountainous snow. It is dangerous but exhilarating to the experienced skier. It is also relatively expensive to rent a helicopter and fly a group to the top of a mountain. The four executives didn't mind paying the $24,000 total price Steve had charged. They figured $6,000 per person was a steal for the thrill of it all.

After the executives had their fill of skiing, Steve herded them into his corporate jet and flew them back to Minnesota. He couldn't help but smile about the trip. As the four young executives were in the aircraft cabin, recounting their thrills of a lifetime, Steve was calculating his profit. A cool $5,500, give or take a few hundred, for just a three-day trip. "Not too shabby of a job," he mumbled to himself. "Not if you call flying airplanes and helicopters work, that is."

He flew toward the eastern horizon with a smile on his face while his clients in the rear of the aircraft toasted their adventure of a lifetime.

* * *

Steve sped down the freeway that led directly to the airport. With the convertible's top down, the wind on that May morning had a bit of a chill at freeway speeds. The spring plant life were showing stages of early growth and, in a few weeks, would be in full bloom.

Steve contemplated how he was going to spend the $75,000 he put in the bank the day before. The crate he was taking to California after his visit to Albert Lea was already secured in the back of his airplane.

He still had questions surrounding the mystery of the deal but was confident nothing illegal was taking place. He had seen a good number of his clients, who were flush with cash, do some fairly odd things.

Although George didn't want a receipt, Steve completed the proper paperwork for transporting the freight. He was going to protect himself regardless of what George at R&D Productions wanted.

He smiled while continuing to reflect on his life. He had come a long way since barnstorming in his dad's two-seater airplane years earlier. He was proud of his flying achievements. Whether the aircraft was a single-engine two-seater, helicopter, or a jet, Steve could fly it. He possessed a natural ability for flying.

His thoughts that morning, like many others, had again turned to his lost love, April. It had been a long time since she walked out of his life, but he still remembered. His memories could still feel her touch, smell her perfume, hear her voice, and see her beautiful eyes. Although he vowed to be done with her four and a half years earlier, he still dreamed of kissing her softly one last time. He wondered where she was and if he would ever see her again.

Tomorrow was to be a special day for the Mitchell family. It was to be the one-hundredth-year reunion day, which was planned several years in advance. Actually, it had started one hundred years earlier by

Steve's great-grandfather Thomas Mitchell. Thomas was his given name, but back then, everyone in his family went by their nicknames. No one could remember what his nickname was and nor did it matter.

Thomas was known as a dreamer in his time. He always thought life held more than what could be seen with the eye. He kept a chest under lock and key for many years near his bed. The story goes that he would place something of value in the chest each year. Steve's family wasn't sure at what age he began doing this, but they do know he continued doing it yearly until his death in 1928, just prior to the stock market crash of 1929.

In his last will and testament, he requested the chest not to be opened until the year 2012. He wanted his descendants of the future, of which he would never meet, to see a piece of the past they would never know.

Through the years, relatives would speculate as to its contents. Visions of treasures danced in everyone's mind, including Steve's. The dusty relic of a chest was kept in the attic at the family homestead in Albert Lea, Minnesota, ninety miles to the south. He remembered sitting on it as a child and pretending it to be a horse. The one-hundredth-year reunion was all about opening dear old Thomas Mitchell's treasure chest.

*   *   *

Steve's dream of flying started as a child with his father's crop-dusting business in Albert Lea. His grandfather Herbert founded the business shortly after World War II with the sizeable inheritance his father, Thomas, had left to him. The Mitchell family was greatly intrigued with the aircraft industry. As a child, Steve heard stories of his grandfather and great-grandfather watching the sky for hours, hoping to get a glimpse of an airplane flying overhead. They both had developed a serious passion for the aircraft industry.

Richard, Steve's father, and Steve's two uncles, Terry and James, were quickly adopted into the family business. They became known as the Flying Mitchell Family. Richard, being the eldest child, was the acting president. Although all too often, it was evident he had no authority over his two younger brothers. Both of them had little respect for their big brother's business leadership and did what they wanted.

Steve's grandfather Herbert was the ultimate authority. Being he was the family patriarch, all three brothers respected him regardless of what they wanted.

Tragedy unexpectedly struck the family back in 1958, several years before Steve was born. His uncle James was killed when the crop duster plane he was piloting clipped a telephone wire over at the Watkins farm. After the accident, Grandpa, they say, was never the same. He blamed himself because he taught James to fly. He felt that possibly the training he gave James wasn't enough. He just could not forgive himself. Thoughts of *maybe I could have done more* danced through his mind.

In 1978, more family tragedy struck. Steve's grandfather, flying well past the age he should have been, made an emergency landing on old Highway 3. He began to have breathing difficulties while ferrying one of the crop dusters to another farm for his sons. Steve's grandmother had been following below in the family pickup. She and a few other motorists immediately stopped and helped him out of the airplane.

Sitting on the pavement, she cradled him in her arms, trying to make him comfortable. Herbert looked into her eyes and said his last words.

"We've had a great life, sweetie. It looks like I'm headed home to be with James. I love you dearly."

With that, he breathed his last breath. Steve's grandmother sobbed quietly while stroking his gray hair.

With barely more than a whisper, she said, "Yes, it has been a good life. Thank you, my darling, and I love you too."

She kissed him one last time and cried.

The tragedy of James's crash left a profound and lasting impact on Steve's father, Richard. Because of it, he insisted Steve join the armed forces and learn the proper way of flying. Richard felt Steve would get better instruction from the military than any flying school could offer. Besides, doing simulated bombing runs was good practice for crop-dusting.

Richard insisted that he and Steve's uncle Terry would carry on the family business until Steve returned from military duty. Richard never did discuss this with him; he just assumed it to be true.

Steve learned his ways for speed by being strapped into an open-cockpit double-wing biplane with his father before he was four years old. Steve remembered his father placing a couple of cloth-covered wooden blocks underneath him so he could see over the side of the airplane. He would then pull the safety harness so tight around his small frame, Steve wanted to cry. Nevertheless, he always managed to give his dad a smile.

His dad would ask him after being firmly strapped in, "Contact, little guy?"

Steve would reply with a boyish charm, "You bettcha!"

Steve loved the thrill of crop-dusting. Flying five feet off the ground at what seemed like the fastest speed imaginable made him smile. He would especially enjoy getting to the end of the field row, and his father would yank back hard on the airplane yoke, making almost a vertical climb. Seconds later, he would throw the yoke to the right and forward, sending the plane almost straight into the ground before pulling straight back hard for another level pass over the field. Steve would squeal at the breathtaking increased speed as they headed for the ground only to level off a few feet above it and head in the opposite direction of which they just came.

The thrill would be repeated over and over until his father was finished with the job.

Steve's childhood was surrounded with flying. He jumped at every chance he could to fly with his father. He too, like his father and grandfather, fell in love with the flying industry.

When Steve was a junior in high school, an air force recruiter came to visit. It was at this time that he decided to follow his father's wishes that he fly in the military. That day after school, Steve and his father discussed the possibilities at length. Richard encouraged his son to pursue his dreams.

After graduating from high school, Steve enrolled at the University of Minnesota to study aeronautical engineering. He studied hard and completed his degree in three and a half years.

Steve joined the air force two weeks after graduating from the university with an advanced ranking because of his degree.

Military life was far different from life on the campus, but he adjusted well. He excelled in all areas and was excited to have the opportunity to fly aircraft as agile as his father's crop-dusting airplanes but were much faster.

While stationed in Maui, Steve earned his helicopter rating. The training and experience would add an essential ingredient to his air-charter service. Steve was trained to fly various other types of aircraft, but the helicopter was the most challenging. Steve's love for flying helped him excel at this too.

*   *   *

Steve exited the freeway next to the airport and pulled his BMW up to the guard shack. The May morning sun radiated heat on Steve's body. The warmth of the sunshine quickly dissipated the chill from the early morning drive. Old Gus came out to greet him.

Gus, a veteran flyer of the Korean War, always had a flying story to tell although his flying days had long passed. His paunchy stomach jiggled as he approached Steve.

"Hey, Mr. Mitchell, how ya doing this morning?" Gus asked in his Southern drawl accent. "Did ya have a great flight over the last couple of days?"

"Great as always," Steve emphatically replied.

"Well, keep it safe today. Kinda cloudy, ya know."

With that, Gus waddled back to the shack and opened the gate. As Steve drove through the gate and into the hangar area, he thought Gus's comment about being safe was a little odd. He had never said that before. Steve shrugged and drove on.

Hangar number 408 housed his 1967 Cessna 310 twin-engine plane. Steve loved this plane more than any other aircraft he had flown. Although it was older, it was still considered a high-performance twin-engine plane and not recommended for the average flight-school trainer. The plane was just too quick and responsive for a student pilot. The responsiveness is what Steve loved best about this plane. He could go out and have some real fun with it.

Trudy was just putting the finishing touches on cleaning the twin-engine plane when Steve drove up to the hangar. He had telephoned her earlier to get the plane ready for a flight to Albert Lea.

Trudy was a full-time student at the University of Minnesota, studying to become an aircraft engineer. Her blue eyes, long blond hair, and slender body contrasted with the soiled coveralls she was wearing over her street clothes that morning. The part-time job Steve gave her, consisting of cleaning and fueling his airplanes, was great for her school schedule. She worked her own hours but occasionally had to ready an aircraft should Steve call, as was the case today.

"All set to go, Mr. Mitchell. Fueled, cleaned inside and out. By the way, I noticed a crate tied down in the back of the plane. What's that for?" Trudy was inquiring about the mysterious crate Steve had previously loaded.

"Ya know, Trudy, it's a long story, and if I told ya, I'd have to kill ya," Steve said laughingly.

Trudy just rolled her eyes back in her head while smiling.

"I have to deliver it to California for a new client after I visit home," Steve explained. "I'll tell you more about it when I get back. Hey, thanks for getting down here on such short notice. I really appreciate you."

"That's okay. It's my job, and I don't mind at all," she replied with a smirk on her face.

Steve knew that Trudy enjoyed being around him. Sometimes he worried that she enjoyed it too much.

"Well, like I said, I do appreciate you. You're a great employee. I'm going to be gone for a few days. I guess you'll have a little time off for your studies," Steve said while beginning to preflight the airplane.

"Fine with me. It's finals week," she said.

She slipped out of the dirty coveralls and, with a wave good-bye, said, "Have a good flight."

She then walked to her car and drove off.

Steve contemplated filing a flight plan with air traffic control, better known as ATC. The pilot weather service earlier had reported a layer of clouds at the 5,500-foot level. Steve figured he could fly at 3,500 feet and would still be within the minimum of visual flying requirements or better known as VFR.

After all, he thought to himself, *Albert Lea is only ninety miles away, thirty-five minutes air time. What possibly could happen?*

He finished his outside preflight inspection, climbed aboard, and buckled himself into the pilot's seat.

Chapter 2

Steve turned his attention to bringing the twin 270-horsepower engines to life. He hesitated and made a sweeping glance at the sky. The weather report he had originally retrieved from his home computer stated a broken cloud layer at 5,500 feet. However, his scan of the sky at the airport told him that it looked fairly thick now. He decided against stopping by the pilot-briefing room at the terminal to obtain a more current weather report. He had seen this same weather pattern many times before and was confident it would not interfere with his flight.

Steve flipped the right engine ignition and auxiliary fuel pump switches to the On position. The auxiliary fuel pump made its usual whirring sound as the electricity from the airplane's two batteries reached it. He pumped the right throttle lever to maximum thrust twice to prime the fuel system for starting. He slid open the small six-inch window just to the left of the pilot's seat. Before turning the right engine ignition switch to the Start position, he leaned over and yelled out the small window opening, "Clear."

The safety procedure was designed to let anyone on the ground know the pilot was about to start the engines and to stand clear of the props.

There was a time when he felt awkward doing this because usually there was no one around the engines when he fired them up. He felt this way until things turned almost tragic one day when Trudy tried to catch him before he left on a flight.

It was a morning like today. He had seen Trudy leave the hangar area in her car while performing his exterior preflight inspection. He had completed the procedure and was in the pilot's seat when the incident happened.

Just after Trudy left the airport, she glanced at her stack of books sitting on the passenger seat of her car. Looking more closely, she realized she had inadvertently picked up the aircraft-maintenance logbook that had been sitting on the counter in the hangar. She knew the logbook was an important part of the aircraft. Being a perfectionist, she did not want Steve to fly without it, so she turned around and headed back to the airport hangar area.

When she got to Gus in the guard shack, she quickly explained the situation to him.

"You better hurry on back to the hangar, little lady. Steve doesn't waste too much time on the ground," Gus told her.

Trudy raced through the entrance and over to hangar number 408. When she arrived, she could see Steve had already completed the exterior preflight inspection and was strapped in the pilot's seat and had already started the right engine. She approached the aircraft from the right side opposite of the pilot because the entry door on the Cessna 310 is located over the right wing just behind the engine. She warily moved closer to the plane. Her long blond hair swirled about her head from the backwash of air coming from the spinning propeller directly in front of her. She gingerly climbed the step on the back of the right wing directly behind the right engine to get to the aircraft door.

Steve was looking to his left when he yelled "Clear" to start the left engine. Just as he was about to hit the ignition switch, Trudy pounded on the door to get his attention. The sudden unexpected noise startled him enough that he jumped and accidentally pushed the right engine throttle controls from idle to near maximum thrust, causing the aircraft to swing wildly to the left.

Although Steve's military training taught him to react quickly to the unexpected, this incident caught him off guard. With the right engine running at such a high rpm, the aircraft had almost completely turned 180 degrees before he could recover it. Almost instantly, Trudy was knocked to the ground from the violent move the plane made. When he finally recovered control, Trudy was sprawled on the pavement with a mere three feet between her and certain death from the wildly spinning propeller.

Steve immediately cut the power to the right engine, unbuckled his seat belt, and bolted out the door, expecting the worst. Trudy was just picking herself off the ground.

Steve tensely asked, "Trudy, are you okay?"

"I . . . I think so."

Then the fear of what had just taken place set in, and she began to cry. Steve gathered her in his arms and held her trembling body for several minutes without a word spoken. Once Trudy had settled down, the two of them talked about the incident and how it could have been avoided. She should have never walked up to the aircraft with the engine running. It would have been better to walk to the front of the aircraft and try to catch Steve's attention. In addition, Steve should have never let the airplane get away from him. His extensive training should not have let the incident happen.

Steve returned from his thoughts back to the flight at hand. With a puff of blue smoke from the exhaust, the right engine sprang to life. He made a quick glance of the gauges to verify everything was operating properly. He noticed the fuel flow pressure gauge to the right engine was registering ten pounds more pressure than normal.

Just last month, it had cost Steve $12,000 to overhaul the right engine to correct that problem.

He had first noticed the fuel pressure gauge begin to rise on a joyride back from Duluth, Minnesota, to the Saint Paul airport. Steve's mechanic, Dan, had suggested the engine overhaul to avoid a meltdown in midair. Steve reluctantly agreed. He was reluctant because of the $12,000 price tag but did not want to err on the side of safety.

It was discovered during the engine rebuild process that sometime earlier in the life of the aircraft, during another engine rebuild, the mechanic at that time used silicone as a gasket sealer. The aircraft mechanic wasn't aware that when aviation fuel comes in contact with the silicone, it breaks down the gasket and causes the remnants to ball up. Eventually, the silicone balls become lodged in the fuel system, causing a restriction in the fuel flow.

Steve wondered if maybe Dan did not get all the silicone out of the system. He watched the fuel flow gauge for several seconds, and it seemed to be stabilized. He decided all looked okay at that point.

He repeated the starting process for the left engine. The fuel gauge was normal for this one. He now was ready to get on with the flight.

"Saint Paul tower, twin Cessna 1144 Quebec ready for taxi," Steve called over the aircraft radio to the airport control tower.

The 1144Q was the aircraft-identification number. Steve was unsure on how the previous owner of his plane had managed to get away with having only four-inch-high lettering for the N-numbers. They were barely visible at a distance. The FAA had standards that called for at least ten-inch-high identification lettering. Nobody ever confronted Steve on the letter height, so he never changed the 1144Q that marked his plane.

Frankly, it made for some fun times. Just this past winter on a Saturday morning, Steve and a group of his friends clambered into the Cessna 310 and flew to Brainerd, Minnesota, for breakfast.

At the south end of town is a popular ice fishing lake called Mille Lacs Lake. Rows of ice fishing houses line the frozen lake and stretch for hundreds of feet at a time, giving the appearance of a miniature city on ice. Many anglers took their sport seriously enough that some of the buildings on the frozen lake came complete with living quarters providing food, heat, and electricity from portable generators for the fishing enthusiast.

After leaving the Brainerd municipal airport, Steve dropped the airplane down to one hundred feet, four hundred feet below the minimum FAA requirement of five hundred feet, and at two hundred miles per hour, buzzed several rows of ice fishing huts. Steve and his guests all had a great laugh as each door on the ice houses would open and anglers, in various stages of dress, bolted from within, each wondering what all the commotion was.

When Steve reached the end of the ice-house rows, he pulled back on the yoke quickly, shooting his Cessna skyward. No one on the ground was able to identify his plane because of the small N-numbers. To this day, talk around the Brainerd airport is that anyone caught buzzing ice houses on the lake will be dealt with severely.

Steve's radio crackled in his headphones. "Twin Cessna 1144 Quebec, taxi at your discretion to runway *one eight* and hold short."

"Twin Cessna 44 Quebec taxi to *one eight* and hold short," Steve replied.

Proper radio etiquette called for the pilot to repeat the highlights of instruction received so the control tower knows the pilot heard them correctly. Only the last two digits of the plane's N-numbers are used when replying.

With his right hand, Steve simultaneously pushed the throttle levers on the center console forward about an inch to increase power to the two engines. The plane lurched forward. Once it was rolling, Steve backed off the throttles a little and headed for the taxiway.

He finally was on his way to Albert Lea, and soon the mysterious crate in the rear of the aircraft would be on its way to California. Steve was going to make a handsome profit on this trip.

Air traffic that morning was very light. Steve noticed one of the local flying-school aircraft doing touch-and-goes on runway 26. He could always recognize the inexperienced student pilots. On landings, the airplane wings would be tipping back and forth on approach. The aircraft would bounce once or twice on the runway and then make a few more sputter bounces and finally settle down. He chuckled at the sight of the landing because he remembered his first flying days doing the same thing.

Steve thought of his first solo flight in an aircraft. It was a small Cessna 172 single-engine aircraft, and as it lifted from the runway, a rush of adrenaline came over him. He was ecstatic to be at the controls without anyone else in the plane. For so many years, he had flown with his father and would occasionally control the plane but only under his father's watchful eye.

Steve approached the end of runway 18 and pulled into the aircraft-parking area to the right of the taxiway. The area was reserved for pilots to do their final checklist and an engine run-up just prior to takeoff. This was the final step before becoming airborne.

Steve pressed firmly on the brakes, then increased the rpm of the left engine to 1,800. He then made a final check of the gauges that told him everything on the left engine was working properly for takeoff. He then completed the same procedure for the right engine.

The fuel flow pressure gauge for the right engine was still indicating a little higher reading than normal. Nevertheless, Steve rationalized that the reading still was the same as during startup, so everything was fine. Besides, he found it hard to believe it could be a problem because Dan was such a good mechanic. He thought it must be a faulty gauge. Steve's confidence in Dan's mechanical ability gave him an assurance that all was okay.

After completing his final checklist and engine run-up, Steve moved the aircraft to the line on the taxiway pavement that separated him from the active runway. Steve keyed the radio microphone. "Saint Paul tower, twin Cessna 1144 Quebec holding short, runway *one eight*, ready for takeoff."

The tower replied, "Twin Cessna 1144 Quebec, clear for takeoff, runway *one eight*, proceed at your discretion, good day."

"Twin Cessna 44 Quebec, clear for takeoff, runway *one eight*, good day," Steve answered back.

After a glance out of the right side of the aircraft to make sure no other aircraft was on final approach for landing, he increased the twin throttles slightly to move into position on the runway. Once the aircraft was lined up on the centerline of the runway, he again applied the brakes. He so enjoyed this part. It was up to him and him alone to put this massive piece of machinery in the air and safely bring it back. As he glanced back and forth over the slightly flexing thirty-eight-foot wingspan, it gave him an awesome sense of responsibility.

The rpm gauges read 1,800. With a quick glance of the oil pressure, fuel pressure indicators, and manifold pressures for positive readings, Steve released the brakes, and the twin-engine plane began its takeoff roll. He pushed the throttles to maximum power for takeoff, gingerly working the foot pedals to keep the aircraft on centerline until he gained enough speed for the aircraft controls to take command.

Twenty miles an hour, all was looking fine. Fifty miles an hour, sixty, eighty, ninety, one hundred miles an hour, one quick systems glance, and it was time to rotate the aircraft off the runway at 105 miles an hour and skyward! Steve pulled back on the aircraft yoke, and the wheels left the ground.

He never failed to have a feeling of exhilaration come over him immediately when the aircraft's landing gear left the runway. Exhilaration but also a little anxiety because on takeoffs, the Cessna 310 aircraft has an uncontrollable dead zone for about two to three seconds after taking off. Because liftoff speed, or better known as rotation speed, was lower than minimum single-engine operating speed, should an engine fail at that time, there was nothing the pilot could do to recover the aircraft. The airplane would simply wing over to the bad engine's side and corkscrew itself into the ground, almost assuring instantaneous death to all aboard.

Steve retracted the landing gear after the plane had cleared the end of the runway. He reduced the throttles from takeoff speed of 2,400 rpm back to cruise range of 1,900 rpm. Three green lights on the instrument panel appeared as the landing gear made a thumping sound, tucking them up under the wings and the nose gear into the fuselage. The aircraft climbed effortlessly to 3,500 feet, Steve's intended cruising altitude. He turned slightly to the right on a heading of 210 degrees. This would take him directly to Albert Lea. In approximately thirty minutes, Steve would be bringing the landing gear back down into place for another smooth landing.

The twin aircraft engines roared as they pulled the weight of the plane through the air, defying gravity. Increasing or decreasing the rpm of each engine would synchronize them so both were pulling evenly. There would be a harmonious whine when both were evenly matched. Steve worked the throttles, moving them ever so slightly until both engines were in perfect tune. He settled in for the short flight.

His mind drifted as the hum of the synchronized engines grumbled. He began thinking of his mom. It had been nearly three months since he had seen her last. She was a short stout woman who seemed to always be wearing a cooking apron. She was an absolutely fabulous cook. When she spoke, her Northern drawl was very evident.

Steve broke into a smile, thinking of her. He missed her so much and was excited to have some time to spend with her. She was such a good mother. He always had the best because his mom wanted that for him.

Several minutes into the flight, Steve looked at the sky with a bit of concern. The cloud deck looked as though it was dropping from the reported 5,500-foot level. Steve decided to radio for an updated weather report.

"Saint Paul tower, twin Cessna 1144 Quebec, requesting current weather."

"Twin Cessna 1144 Quebec, current weather is Kilo, current altimeter setting is 29.11, solid layer at flight level 45," came the reply.

"Saint Paul tower, twin Cessna 44 Quebec has Kilo, good day."

The aviation industry gives names to the weather reports in alphabetical succession. This is done so the pilot knows whether he or she has the correct weather settings. Steve updated his altimeter setting from 30.25 to the new setting of 29.11. Changing the pressure setting on the altimeter allowed the gauge to report the aircraft's true altitude.

The weather report he had left with was named Juliet. The cloud deck was scattered at 5,500 feet at that time. In the short time that Steve had been airborne, the cloud layer had thickened and dropped one thousand feet! He knew something was brewing with the weather. The blackening clouds told him a storm was developing right on top of him.

He debated whether to turn around and return to Saint Paul or keep pushing hard and beat the storm to Albert Lea. He finally listened to better judgment and turned left to return to the Saint Paul airport. Before completing the 180-degree turn, Steve realized that the weather had closed in behind him as well as in front of him. The clouds looked as though they reached to the ground where the airport was supposed to be. He now knew that his best chances were to keep heading for Albert Lea. His overconfident flying nature caused him to leave without proper planning and now had put him in a tense situation.

Steve sighed in disgust at his previous lack of concern for following procedures as he watched the cloud deck get lower and lower. Many times during his flight training, he was warned of pilot overconfidence. He vowed it would never happen to him, and yet here he was, facing a situation that was a true-to-life form of pilot overconfidence.

He knew he soon would be flying by instruments without filing the proper flight plan. The clouds were thickening too quickly. He had to contact air traffic control to get an instrument clearance into the Albert Lea airport.

"Saint Paul tower, twin Cessna 1144 Quebec requesting IFR clearance to Albert Lea."

"Twin Cessna 1144 Quebec, contact Des Moines on 114.3, good day," came the tower's reply.

"Des Moines on 114.3, Twin Cessna 44 Quebec, good day."

Before Steve had the opportunity to change the radio frequency to Des Moines Air Traffic Control, a sickening metal screech came from the right engine. At the same time, he could feel the plane start to pull to the right.

"Uh-oh, what's happening here?" he said aloud to himself.

He glanced at the instrument panel in front of him. The temperature on the right engine was pegged at the red warning mark on the gauge. Fuel pressure and oil pressure had already dropped to zero.

Steve had an unsettling feeling, realizing he had a major malfunction in his right engine. He immediately started his emergency procedures. He stepped on the left rudder pedal, and it was like stepping on a soft grapefruit. That confirmed it; he had a complete failure of the right engine. Steve continued the emergency procedure of feathering the props on the engine to minimize the drag on the aircraft.

Sweat began to bead on his forehead. He had lost an engine or two in the military, but those were jet engines. Each had so much thrust that you could strap one to a bathtub and it would fly. However, this was different. A twin-engine propeller-driven aircraft doesn't have that much climbing power with one engine disabled. Steve was now flying in the clouds with only one engine operational!

His heart beat faster with the next sound he heard. The left engine now began to misfire. Steve looked at the fuel gauges, but all registered nearly full.

He wondered why the only remaining engine is sputtering. He quickly started the emergency procedures he had practiced so many times.

With a glance to the left engine's fuel flow gauge, he knew he had a serious problem. The fuel flow gauge indicator was all over the place. It would jump to thirty pounds per square inch and then back down to five and continued to flutter back and forth.

Steve came to the quick conclusion that maybe the right fuel pressure gauge wasn't faulty and was reading correctly. Some of the old silicone gasket pieces must have remained in the system and were more than likely causing the problem. That was probably what destroyed the right engine, and now the left engine was on the verge of catastrophic failure. Steve surmised that somehow the remaining silicone had worked its way through the fuel system and into the left engine. *But how?* he wondered. *There are redundant systems to catch contaminated fuel!* Suddenly, there was a strange, eerie silence. Only the wind passing over the aircraft could be heard. The left engine had now failed completely. Steve quickly reached for the ignition switch. He gave it a quick turn to the left, but the engine refused to come to life. Again, he tried it, and again no response. Several times he tried to refire the left engine while the aircraft continued its descent toward the ground.

Steve finally gave up on starting the failed engine and turned his attention toward an emergency crash landing of his airplane. He feathered the props and checked his altitude and speed. He could not let the aircraft speed fall below ninety-five miles an hour, or it would go into a flat spin, causing it to fall from the sky completely uncontrollable. He tried to reach for the radio to send a Mayday, but he had his hands full, trying to control a lifeless airplane.

His altitude had now dropped below the cloud deck. He continued looking below for a clearing to make an emergency landing. All he saw were trees everywhere he looked! Steve kept hoping to find an opening to make an emergency landing.

Steve was too busy handling the five thousand pounds of airplane to be nervous. His altitude had dropped to five hundred feet now. Just barely visible up ahead was the river. That was his only hope. He was going to have to ditch the airplane in the river. Now if he could only make the water.

Steve kept the plane hovering near the ninety-five-miles-an-hour stall speed.

"Come on, baby, you can do it! Come on, stay afloat a little longer for me." Steve was talking to his plane as if it were a person.

The trees looked too close now. He felt he could reach out and grab the treetops.

There was a brilliant flash of white light and the tearing of metal from the right wing. Things now began to move in slow motion for Steve. The white light came from the right wingtip's fuel tank being sheared off by an exceptionally tall and strong northern pine. The fifty gallons of aviation fuel quickly ignited into a ferocious ball of angry white-hot flames. Steve's altitude had dropped too low. He was now in the middle of a dreaded airplane crash.

Surprisingly, he felt calm, as if he were watching it all happen on a movie screen. *This isn't happening*, he kept thinking. The seat belt pulled hard against his body as the plane made the abrupt transition from air to ground. He felt the pain of his seat belt snap and himself being hurled through the front windshield. Odd things were going through his mind at this time. He thought, *How is it possible to fit through that small windshield opening?* He also thought about the crate in the rear of the aircraft.

Silence broke out in the forest as Steve's plane disintegrated around him. By now, he was not entirely aware of his surroundings. He could feel the heat from the fire as it burned around him. Steve fell into a deep trance as he lay seventy-five feet from the closest part of the plane, or what was left of it. The fire burned the last remaining part of Steve's beloved aircraft, twin Cessna 1144 Quebec.

Chapter 3

The sun glistened softly through the tree branches. The forest was exceptionally quiet. A bird whistled for a mate in the background. A gentle breeze rustled the leaves. Steve was trying to decide if he was dead or alive. The storm that had surrounded him during the crash was now replaced with a tranquil setting of a cloudless sky.

He soon discovered he was very much alive by the excruciating pain he felt when he attempted to move. It was evident his right leg and right arm were broken. Moving increased the pain through his body like he had never felt before. Most of his clothing had been ripped away during the crash. All he had left on was the jeans he had been wearing when he took off; however, they were now badly ripped and torn. Thankfully, he was thrown clear of the burning wreckage. He had no burn marks—just cuts, abrasions, and broken bones.

He wondered how long he had been unconscious. The last thing he remembered was the sudden thrust he felt as he was being propelled through the front windshield of the plane.

Steve groaned as he thought about where his plane was—or what was left of it.

With a much-painful effort, he positioned himself so he was sitting with his back against a white birch tree. He gazed to where he thought the wreckage should be. There was nothing to be seen except the forest undergrowth and trees.

I don't know where I'm at. It has to be nearby, he thought to himself.

He strained to look in all directions but discovered no sign of a plane crash. No damage to the trees or even a gouge in the ground could be seen. This was becoming all too unreal to Steve. He began to think that maybe he didn't survive and that he now was in some sort of afterlife setting. The crash, as he remembered, was horrendous before he blacked out. There should be wreckage strewn about a large area. However, there was nothing. Not a scrap of paper, clothing, metal—any evidence to indicate there was a plane crash.

Steve slipped in and out of consciousness. He wondered if a search and rescue operation would find him soon enough. He knew they would find the wreckage but wondered if they would find him before his injuries killed him.

His world was now going dark again. Steve was still scanning his surroundings, hoping to find his plane, when his senses shut down. He could still hear the bird in the background, but it too slowly faded away.

*　*　*

Pierce yelled, "Over this way, Tommy. I know the river is this way!"

"Are you sure, Pierce? Because this thing is getting heavier and heavier to drag, and I don't want to turn around again," Tommy replied.

The two eleven-year-old school friends were on a mission to sail a raft on the mighty Mississippi River. They had tried to reach the river last week but failed. The spring runoff from the harsh winter of that year, 1863, had caused the forest undergrowth to thicken and grow tall. After walking and dragging the raft for almost an hour through the thick underbrush, both had lost interest in finding the river that day. They had given up and returned home, planning to try again soon.

Their interest in the river was piqued in their adventurous spirit when a band of gypsies came through their hometown of Newport, Minnesota. The gypsies arrived in town at midday about six weeks ago with their horse-drawn wagons filled with trinkets and tonics. Word spread quickly around town about their arrival. Weaving in and around people, Tommy and Pierce raced down to Main Street when they heard all the commotion.

The two of them worked their way to the front of the crowd to hear the stories being told. Both heard about fabulous sights and adventures downstream on the mighty Mississippi River from the group of nomads.

Being both of them were mischievous eleven-year-olds, they listened wide-eyed and in awe. Both rushed home to tell their parents of the things they had heard. The reception of their newfound adventure was not quite what they had expected.

Pierce's mother, Anna May, was a single parent. His father was killed in a drunken brawl when Pierce was only five years old, leaving his mother to raise four kids. Pierce's older brother by seven years, Matthew, was left to become the head of the household. He also had two younger sisters, Missy and Susan, who were ages three and one at the time of their father's unexpected death. Anna May had her work cut out for her in raising the four children.

Pierce, because of his age, fell in the middle regarding his siblings. His mother was busy caring for the younger two, and his older brother was trying to find work to help put food on the table. Pierce was left to attend to himself most of the time, but his mother still kept a watchful eye on him. She knew he had an adventurous streak in him and that it could easily lead to mischief.

Tommy had both of his parents. He spent a good deal of time on Main Street because his father, Samuel, was the local blacksmith. Tommy was the youngest of three children. He had two older twin brothers, Michael and Walter. Both would continually tease Tommy because of his vivid imagination. Tommy certainly could dream up some wild stories. The two older brothers bestowed the nickname of Dreamer on him. It never bothered Tommy because he enjoyed being lost in his world of make-believe.

Tommy and Pierce were inseparable. The family homesteads were next to each other, and the two of them became like brothers. They were always into mischief.

When the two of them came home to tell of their grand idea of rafting the river—well, it wasn't going to happen, according to Anna May and Tommy's mother, Abigail.

"The river is just too dangerous," both mothers scolded.

* * *

Tommy and Pierce stopped for a moment to rest from dragging the homebuilt raft they had constructed in secret. Their plan was to sail the mighty Mississippi River. Neither boy's parents were aware of the scheme the two had concocted.

Both boys had plenty of warning about the dangers of the river. The currents were swift and cold from the melting snow up north. The harsh winter and warm spring season brought about a torrent of rushing water. It seemed to pool in every low spot as far as the eye could see.

Tommy leaned against a tree to catch his breath. His eyes scanned the ravine hollow below. He was wondering how hard it was going to be to get the raft back up the other side. Pierce was sitting on a large rock, casting pebbles at the ground.

He sighed and asked, "Tommy, what do you think we will find downriver?"

"Ah shucks, I don't know. But I sure want to find out."

Pierce continued his questioning. "Do ya suppose we'll be able to get back home after we find whatever we're gonna find?"

Tommy just looked at him with a blank stare. He had focused so much on rafting the river, he hadn't given a thought on how to get back home. The adventure loomed too big in his mind to be rational about its ending.

Tommy, ignoring Pierce's question, looked back toward the ravine. His gaze stopped as he focused on a small colorful clump of what looked like clothing sticking out from behind a tree at the bottom of the ravine.

"Look at that!" Tommy said. "I think someone is sitting down by that tree."

Pierce rose from the rock where he was sitting and looked in the direction Tommy was pointing.

"Where?"

"Over there!" Tommy exclaimed.

"I see it!" Pierce said with squinted eyes. "You're right. I think that's somebody just sitting there. He sure is sitting still. Do ya suppose he's hunting?" Pierce asked.

"I don't know," Tommy answered.

The boys decided to get a better look. They left the raft on top of the ridge and slowly worked their way down the side of the ravine. Tommy led the way. The hearts of both boys were pounding. Very few people lived near here and even fewer ventured into the woods headed for the river. Who was this person and what was he doing sitting in a ravine were questions that danced in both of their minds.

As they got closer, they could see the man was sitting motionless. His clothes were badly torn. His left shoulder protruded beyond the tree. The two boys could see that a thick layer of skin had been peeled back on the man's shoulder. Flies and ants had infested the pulpy mass. Dried and fresh blood were coating the man's arm to his wrist. The wound still oozed a small stream of fresh blood. The boys could see the man was badly hurt.

The two boys slowly moved around to the front of him. His right leg from the thigh down was cocked abnormally to the outside. The boys could clearly see it was broken. About an inch of the broken thighbone had penetrated the muscle and skin and could be seen extending from the tear in his pants. A lone fly darted back and forth around the bone tip. Numerous cuts surrounded the right side of his head. Dirt and leaves had matted themselves to the seepage that had come from his cuts and scrapes.

Tommy moved closer.

"Mister . . . mister."

Tommy was trying to arouse a response from the man.

"Can you hear me?" Tommy asked.

The rescue team Steve had hoped for didn't arrive. No fancy medications and no state-of-the-art hospital were going to help Steve recover now. Instead two boys, Tommy and Pierce, happened upon him, and the year was 1863!

Steve heard the voice of Tommy, and he tried to talk but could only manage an almost inaudible groan. He was barely alert to his surroundings.

"Tommy, do you think he's alive?" Pierce asked.

"Yeah, I think so. I saw his hand move," he replied.

Tommy leaned in toward Steve for a better look. "I think someone has beat him up real good."

Steve could see slightly through his swollen eyes that two figures were standing in front of him. In an almost incoherent state of pain, he realized he finally had been found. Steve could not communicate anything because of his severe injuries. Soon he drifted off into a darkened world of blackness. His senses had shut down again.

Pierce looked at Tommy and then compassionately looked back at Steve.

Pierce spoke first. "Tommy, why don't you stay here, and I'll go get help. That way you can yell so I know where ya are."

Tommy agreed. "Okay, Pierce, but hurry."

Pierce turned and ran up the incline through the brush toward town.

Tommy maneuvered a broken tree trunk over to Steve. He sat on the stump with a sense of alarm. He was definitely nervous. He had not seen anyone look this beat-up since his friend Ray was trampled by a bull. Tommy continued to wonder who this man was and where he came from.

"Mister . . . mister, can you hear me?" Tommy asked.

Steve heard nothing. His mind was blank. Not hurting and not feeling, he was in a world of nothingness. Tommy continued to sit, nervously looking in all directions. It was a bit scary to be sitting there all alone.

He whispered softly to himself, "Please hurry back, Pierce."

Chapter 4

Pierce retraced his steps as he ran through the woods. His heart was pounding over what he had just experienced. He thought about his friend, Tommy, sitting back with that man.

Where did he come from? Who could help him? Where is his family?

All these thoughts were filling his mind as he ran as hard as he could for help. The thought of Tommy being alone with a stranger was beginning to scare Pierce. He was wondering whether whoever beat up the man would return and harm Tommy.

The fear Pierce was experiencing caused him to race even harder through the woods. Instead of turning right onto the path that led to town, he turned left and headed for the home of his schoolteacher, Jean. He was fearful to go home with the news because of the warnings he and Tommy had received about going to the river.

Jean was an exceptionally beautiful woman with brown eyes and brunette hair. No one knew her age for sure because she looked much younger than her actual age of thirty-eight. She worked hard to keep her youthful look.

Although she was the prettiest single woman in the area, Jean had never married. Two years earlier, her fiancé had left for the East Coast for some further governmental studies, and she never heard from him again except for a telegram she received that said he would not be returning to Minnesota. She surmised he probably met some eastern woman that wooed his heart away.

Her heart was broken for a while, but then she determined it was time to get on with life and let her hopes of him returning fade. There were plenty of local single men who tried hard to be part of her life, but none lived up to her standards. She would become bored with them within a short time. She wanted more out of life. She longed for romance and adventure. She wanted a man who would sweep her off her feet with intellect, wit, and humor. She wanted him to be confident and strong in his nature. She didn't think she would ever find this type of man, so she resolved to herself that she would live alone for the rest of her life.

Fear had so gripped Pierce that when he finally arrived at Jean's home, he bolted through the open door as if being chased by a wild animal. It so startled Jean, the eggs she had collected and placed in her apron dropped to the floor of the cabin.

"For heaven's sake, lad, what has gotten into you?" she scolded.

Jean bent down to try and clean the mess Pierce had caused her to make.

"I'm sorry, Ms. Jean, but Tommy and I need your help!" Pierce breathlessly blurted.

Jean was still in a crouched position near the floor, picking up the mess as she looked up at the boy. She could see he was greatly disturbed. The corners of his mouth were pulled back in a grimace, and his eyes were glassy with fear.

"What's happened?" Jean asked with great concern.

She was fearful that someone in either boy's family had been hurt. She only had eighteen kids in her one-room school, and she taught every grade. The same kids would return each school year, so she got to know all of them and their families well. She knew Tommy and Pierce were great friends, and she knew the mischief they would often get into.

Pierce began to piece the story together for Jean. He was breathing heavily as he tried to speak. The run to Jean's cabin had taken his breath away.

"Tommy and I were going to the river and—"

Jean cut him off in midsentence because she feared the worst.

She quickly asked, "Pierce, you know you are not to go there! Is Tommy okay?"

"Yeah, he's okay. We never made it to the river. We had just cleared the south ridge and were resting when Tommy saw something down below. We could see it was a man. It scared us at first, but then we got curious about who was down there. We hiked to the bottom, and we could see a man just sitting against a tree, not moving. He looked real bad. Someone beat him up so much, he couldn't move."

Jean was listening intently now.

"Well, where's Tommy?" she asked.

"We wanted to help him, so Tommy stayed with him while I went to get help. He is going to yell when he hears me coming so we know where to find them. Can you come and help him? Please, *please*?" Pierce pleaded.

"You two boys can sure cause a ruckus! I'll gather a few things, and we'll go. But first I want you to go home and tell your ma where you're at," Jean said sternly.

"But, Ms. Jean, if I go home, my ma will be sore at me, and I'm the only one who knows where Tommy is, and it will be dark soon. I promise to go right home after I show you where the man is. Please, can I show you now? Tommy is out there alone with him, and I'm afraid something will happen to him," Pierce continued to plead.

"Okay." Jean sighed. "I suppose it is getting late, and I don't want you two out after dark. Let me get my medical supplies."

Jean grabbed a small leather bag from beside her bed that contained various medical supplies. Doc Green, who came down from the city, visited every so often and left the medical supplies with Jean to take care of cuts, scrapes, and abrasions the kids at school would invariably get. She wasn't sure if these supplies would be enough. This sounded serious.

"Pierce, can the man walk?" Jean asked.

"I don't think so. His leg looks pretty broken," Pierce responded.

Jean thought that as long as Pierce was with her, she might as well bring some supplies to make the man comfortable. If it was true that the man had a broken leg, there wouldn't be enough time to get him out of the woods before nightfall. He most likely would have to spend the night right where he was. Jean had not had much experience with broken bones, but she had enough to know that it was not as easy as washing a cut and putting a dressing on it.

"Pierce, grab those blankets over there and a couple of handfuls of the dried beef on the shelf. Is there water nearby?"

"Yeah, I think so. I'm pretty sure we were almost to the river," Pierce answered.

"Good. Grab that larger canteen hanging on the wall," she instructed.

Pierce reached for the canteen, swung it over his shoulder, and stopped.

He turned to Jean and in a soft voice said, "Ms. Jean, thank you for helping."

Jean momentarily stopped from rushing around and gathering the things she thought she would need. She bent down and looked at Pierce tenderly. She had such bad luck with love in her own life, but she knew her students loved her as a mother, and she loved them as if they were her own children.

Her passion for teaching went beyond the classroom. She wanted to impart to them the knowledge they would need to live and work in a world that seemed to be changing. The turn of the century was going to happen in their lifetime, and she wanted them to be prepared for it. Not only prepared in book knowledge, but in life's lessons as well.

She looked into the blue eyes of the blond-headed little boy and said in a motherly voice, "Pierce, first of all, you know what your ma and Tommy's parents have said about going to the river. You have to learn that obedience to your parents is the first lesson in life. However, the second lesson in life is when you learn to help others. You did wrong by going to the river when you weren't supposed to, but you did right by trying to help someone in need. I am sure this person, whoever he is, appreciates the fact that you both did not run away from him. We are going to help him first, and then you and Tommy are going to have to face the consequences of your actions. Do you understand that?"

Pierce looked at the floor and, with a shuffling of his feet, simply said, "I know."

"Okay then, I think we have everything. Let's go do life lesson number two and help this guy out."

*   *   *

"Tommy . . . Tommy!" Pierce called out. "We came this way, Ms. Jean. We were at the top of this ridge when we saw the man. Tommy!" Pierce yelled again.

"Pierce, let's go down a little further on the ridge. It looks like there is a place we can see a little better," Jean told him.

By now, she too was calling Tommy's name.

"There it is, there it is! There's our raft. We're close now. Tommy!" Pierce called out again.

"Down here!" Tommy excitedly replied.

Tommy turned toward Steve and said, "Mister, I don't know if you can hear me, but help is here!"

Pierce and Jean hurried down the hill toward Tommy's voice. As the two of them broke into the clearing, the boys smiled brightly at each other. Tommy was glad Jean came. He knew she would know what to do.

Jean looked at Steve with concern. "Boys, this guy looks terrible. He's lucky you two didn't run in the opposite direction."

She knelt next to Steve and examined his injuries.

"Okay, boys, I want you to gather some firewood. This guy isn't going anywhere tonight. I am going to tend to him right here for now. His injuries are going to need some fixing before we try to move him out of here. While you two gather the wood, I'm going to the river and get some water." Jean asked Pierce, "Would you please hand me that canteen you carried down here?" Pierce swung the canteen from his shoulder and handed it to Jean.

"Ms. Jean, do you want Pierce and me to stay the night with you?" Tommy asked.

"No, Tommy, I'll be fine. I don't want your parents to worry about you two. Besides, I don't think he'll be giving me much trouble," she told the two boys as she looked back at Steve and his injuries.

Jean swung the canteen over her shoulder and headed for the river. She pushed through the brush while Tommy and Pierce stayed behind and gathered the firewood that Jean would need for the night. Her thoughts turned toward the injured man and how mystified she was with him. She could see through his injuries that he was very attractive. She wondered if he was an educated man and if he was a gentleman.

Jean worked her way down the cliff overlooking the river to get to the river's edge. Once there, she filled the canteen with cool water from the river. She found herself in a hurry to get back to the injured man. The whole ordeal was beginning to turn into an adventure, and like the two boys, Jean had a fondness for adventure.

Tommy and Pierce already had a nice fire going when she returned with the water.

"Thanks, boys. I think that should be enough wood for the night. Now I want the both of you to head on home and tell your parents about this. Also, Tommy, would you have your father bring a wagon back here in the morning? I think this guy will be able to make the journey by then. Well," she paused, "at least to my place. Now hurry along. It's getting late."

Tommy and Pierce headed up the hill and toward home. Each was a little nervous. Not for Jean being alone with the man but because they were going to have to confess their whereabouts.

Jean turned to Steve. Putting her hands on her hips, she wondered where to begin. "Mister, you sure are a mess," she said to herself with a challenge in her voice.

She decided the first thing to do was to clean up his wounds. Jean knelt down next to Steve with her bag of medical supplies and the canteen of water. She took a cloth from the bag and soaked it with water. Although Steve was unconscious, Jean deliberately went slowly to minimize any discomfort he may have felt. As she worked the cloth over his chest, she could feel the firmness of his muscles with each breath he took. The feel of his rigid upper-body form intrigued her.

Jean finished washing the dirt and dried blood from his head, chest, arms, and legs. She could see his forearm was protruding forward and had a slight twist to it. She could see it was definitely broken. His leg was also badly fractured.

Jean whispered aloud, "Well, Mr. Whoever You Are, other than a few cuts and abrasions, it looks like the most serious are the broken arm and leg."

Jean reached into her bag and pulled out a brown-colored bottle. Jean pulled the cork from the top. She could handle cuts and scrapes, but she knew she was going to have to set the broken bones. That made her a little squeamish because this wasn't the usual doctoring she was accustomed to.

She decided a good shot of whiskey would help take the edge off. She raised the bottle to her lips and tilted it skyward. The whiskey definitely had a burn to it as the liquid flooded the inside of her mouth. She set the bottle down at her side and wiped her mouth on the cuff of her sleeve. She went over to where the boys had stacked the firewood for her and pulled four straight pieces from the pile. Next, she took a rag and tore it into strips.

"Okay, mister, I think it's time to set those broken bones."

She took another quick swig from her whiskey bottle. She decided to start first with his arm. With one quick jerk and a twist to the right, Jean set the broken bone in his arm. She took two of the sticks and placed them on either side of his arm to make a splint. Holding them in place, she firmly wrapped the cloth around the splint. Steve's right hand began to convulse slightly. His body was reacting to the pain although he was unconscious. She wrapped it tightly to ensure his arm was immobilized.

"There, that should hold it. Now time to work on that leg."

Jean swallowed hard. The bone protruding from the skin unnerved her a bit, but she refrained from taking another swallow of whiskey.

Jean grasped Steve's leg firmly around the knee area and pulled on it steadily. The wound around the area where the bone had broken the skin made a suction sound as the thighbone disappeared back into its place. She worked the bone back and forth and from side to side to make sure it was properly set. She could feel the vibration of the bones scraping against each broken end. When she was convinced it was in its proper place, she straddled his leg and used her knees to hold the splint sticks in place while she wrapped his leg up firmly.

Jean was thankful the man was not awake to feel the setting of his broken bones. The ordeal already had made her a little nauseous, and if he was awake, Jean was not sure she would be able to handle him hollering in pain.

She took advantage of his loss of consciousness to lay him down next to the tree he was leaning against. She rolled one of the blankets she and Pierce had brought and placed it under his head. With another, she covered him up to give him warmth. The night air was beginning to get a bit of a nip to it. Jean curled up in a blanket directly across from him and watched him breathe.

Where was he from? How did he get here? Who was he? What did he do? These were questions racing through Jean's mind. They would have to be answered later because for now, the man was not able to explain himself. She would have to be content with just trying to get some sleep. However, sleep did not come quickly. She continued thinking about the man on the other side of the campfire.

*   *   *

Pierce and Tommy raced up the path toward home. When they got to the clearing just before the two family homesteads, they stopped to catch their breath and to talk. It was late, and the sun had already started to slip beneath the horizon.

"Tommy, what are we gonna tell our folks?" Pierce asked.

"I suppose I could tell them we just wanted to look at the river."

Pierce agreed. "Yeah, we don't have to tell them about the raft. We'll get a whipping for sure!"

The boys stood for a moment in silence and to catch their breath.

"Well, see you in the morning, Pierce."

With that, Tommy turned to go up the path to his home, and Pierce continued straight to his.

*   *   *

Abigail, Tommy's mother, was just beginning to serve dinner to Tommy's two older brothers, Michael and Walter, when Tommy bolted through the door.

"Where ya been, Tommy?" Michael asked in a sarcastic voice.

"Probably off in a dreamworld again," Walter chimed in. "And, Tommy, what distant land were you off to today? Did ya fight the bad guys and win?" he jokingly asked.

Both boys were now laughing and making fun of little Tommy. He just pulled up a chair and sat down at the table, trying to ignore the teasing his two older brothers were doing.

Tommy's mother scolded the two older siblings. "Boys, stop teasing your brother. You both should be so lucky to have such an imagination. A mind is a terrible thing to waste. Tommy, I want you to wash up before you sit at the table. You're as filthy as can be. Go on now. Get it done," Abigail instructed him.

Tommy removed himself from the table and went to the basin in the corner. He grabbed the pitcher of water and filled the basin with enough water to wash his arms too. His mother was right. He did get awful dirty carrying that raft and gathering firewood for Ms. Jean.

Tommy returned to the table all cleaned up. His mother had poured him a bowl of the beef stew she had made. It was his favorite.

"So, Tommy," his mother said in passing, "how in the world did you get so dirty today?"

Tommy paused before answering. "Ma, does it help make wrong right if you help somebody while you're doing wrong?"

"Son, wrong is wrong and right is right, and the two never go hand in hand. Why would you ask such a question?"

"Well . . ." Tommy paused to take a spoonful of stew. "Pierce and I wanted to see the river. We heard so much about it that we just had to see for ourselves," Tommy said hurriedly.

Michael and Walter began to taunt Tommy.

"You're gonna get in trouble. You're gonna get in trouble," they both chanted.

"Boys, stop that!" Abigail snapped. She turned toward Tommy and sternly said, "Tommy, your father and I have repeatedly told you to stay away from that river. It is far too dangerous for little boys to be around. When your father comes home, we're going to have to discuss some disciplinary measures."

Tommy pleaded with her. "But, Ma, I haven't told you what happened. We never made it to the river. At the bottom of the ridge, we found a man that had been beaten up real bad."

His two older brothers were getting set to give him another blast of good old-fashioned teasing when Abigail interrupted. "Thomas Lee, all the more reason not to go to the river. Not only is the river dangerous, but you never know what strangers are lurking about down there."

Her voice told all the boys that she wasn't at all happy with what Tommy was saying.

Just then, the door opened, and in walked Tommy's father, Samuel. He was a huge man with a burly appearance. Being a blacksmith all his life had weathered his appearance greatly. Before he had a chance to wash up, Abigail relayed the story about Tommy going to the river. Although Samuel had a rough look to him, he was as gentle as a lamb but still stern. The boys knew they had better respect him at all times.

He walked over to where Tommy was sitting, stood over him with each hand firmly planted on his hips, and looked down at him.

"Number one," he stated slowly, "you were told not to go to the river. However, you did it anyway. I assume Pierce went with you?" he asked of Tommy.

"Yes, sir," came Tommy's reply.

"So in other words, you said, 'Pa, I'm not going to do what you say. I'm going to do what I want.'"

"No, Pa," Tommy sheepishly replied.

Samuel continued, "Well, that's what your actions said you did, and for disobeying me, your punishment will be to stack the firewood your two brothers split yesterday."

The two older brothers cracked huge smiles because they had escaped the chore of stacking the firewood for the next winter. It was a tremendous job.

Samuel continued, "Secondly, I understand you found someone beat-up out there. Where is this man now?"

"We ran to Ms. Jean's cabin for help because she is always doing the doctoring when Doc Green is gone. She came to where we found the man, and she was going to fix him up. She asked if you could bring a wagon from the shop tomorrow morning to get him out of the woods."

Samuel answered, "As I said, son, the river is off-limits, and you have to be punished for going there. As far as this man you found beat-up, well, I guess you did the right thing in getting help for him. But you shouldn't have been there in the first place. I'll go to the shop in the morning, get the wagon, and we can go get this guy."

Tommy agreed with everything his father had said. During the rest of dinner, Tommy sat in silence. He thought about the man in the woods. He also thought about the woodpile. It was huge!

*   *   *

The full moon shown through the trees as darkness replaced the dusk. The fire sparkled in Jean's eyes. She continued thinking of this man who seemed to have come from nowhere. He had a rugged, handsome appearance that was appealing to her. She found herself wanting to talk to him. She wanted to know who he was and where he came from. The longer she stared at him, the more fascinated she became.

Steve gave a groan as the effects of his injuries tormented his senses. Suddenly, he let out a loud cry, "Pull up! Pull up!"

Jean jumped up and moved to his side. She took a wet cloth and wiped his forehead, trying to calm him.

"Easy, sir, you've been hurt pretty bad. You're going to have to be strong to fight the pain," Jean softly whispered.

Steve could hear distant words but couldn't put anything together. His extreme pain kept his mind from rationalizing anything. He just knew he hurt and was in trouble. He wanted to talk, but his mouth and mind would not work together coherently. All he seemed to be able to do was groan in pain.

Jean asked him as she continued to wipe his forehead with the wet cloth, "Mister, can you hear me? Mister . . . mister?"

There was no response from her questioning.

"Mister, I'm not sure if you can hear me, but hang in there. We're going to get you out of here in the morning."

The campfire illuminated the sincerity in Jean's beautiful brown eyes. Her appearance would make him feel at ease and confident that she would listen to his story. It would be an intense story that would be so far from being believable, Steve would have a hard time believing it himself. He would have to convince himself that he was far from home and the comfortable life he lived in the year 2012. Somehow, he would have to accept it was now 1863 and the lifestyle it held.

The full moon now had cleared the trees and illuminated the small clearing where Jean tended to Steve's injuries. An owl could be heard deep within the forest. Jean repositioned Steve's blanket to cover his shoulders because the night air was becoming cooler. She moved herself closer to where Steve rested. She tried to sleep but was only able to doze periodically. She was concerned about the man she was trying to help. In her mind, she questioned what the morning dawn would bring. Would she help Samuel load the man in the wagon and head for home, or would she help dig the man's grave? It made for a long night in the woods.

Chapter 5

Tommy's mom had just finished cooking eggs and pork for breakfast as Tommy entered the room.

"Where's Pa?" he asked excitedly.

"He's in town, picking up the wagon to go get this man you two found. He'll be back shortly," she said.

Tommy sat down at the table and began to eat rapidly.

"Slow down, young man. You act like you have a fire in your pants!" Abigail scolded.

"I'm sorry. I just want to be ready to go when Pa comes back with the wagon," Tommy said.

"Tommy! Tommy!"

Pierce could be heard hollering from outside Tommy's cabin door.

"Come on in, Pierce."

Pierce was a little reluctant to enter because he knew how much trouble he had gotten into for trying to go to the river, and he was unsure of how things were in Tommy's household.

"Pierce, would you like some breakfast?" Abigail asked.

"Sure would!"

Pierce didn't hesitate to answer. He was around quite often and was almost like family, and he loved Abigail's cooking.

"Well, scoot yourself on up to the table," she told him. Pierce sat down while Abigail placed a plate full of food in front of him.

Again, Pierce didn't hesitate to eat. He left his cabin in a hurry and didn't take time to eat very much. He was anxious to see his friend Tommy and swap stories on what kind of trouble the both of them had gotten into for attempting to go to the river.

The two boys whispered among themselves as Abigail attended to chores on the far side of the room.

"So, Tommy, what happened last night with you?" Pierce quietly asked.

"Ma was really upset with me, and Pa is going to make me stack all the firewood my brothers cut."

He asked Tommy if he had gotten a whipping.

"Naw, just a good talking to and the big firewood chore to do," Tommy answered. "How about you? What happened with your ma?"

"She made me sit in the corner for a bit and go without eating. I sure am glad your ma asked me if

I wanted breakfast. I was getting pretty hungry," Pierce said.

Just as the boys were finishing, the pounding of horse hoofs could be heard coming up the path.

"That must be my pa! Let's head out and meet him so we can get going," Tommy said.

Pierce jumped up to follow Tommy.

"Hold up just a minute there, you two. I want each of you to clean up all the food on your plate," Abigail called to the two from the other side of the room.

Both boys scooped huge spoonfuls of eggs and pork into their mouths. One last swig of milk and they dashed out the door just as Samuel was coming up the path with the wagon from his shop in town. He decided to use a team of horses to pull the wagon rather than just a single horse. He knew the terrain toward the river was hilly, and he didn't want to put such a strain on a single horse.

Samuel brought the team to a stop in front of the cabin.

"Boys, I want you to move those extra hitches in the wagon to one side and spread a layer of hay in there to make it more comfortable for this guy," Samuel instructed the boys.

He climbed the steps to the cabin, stopped, and turned back toward the boys.

"Oh, one more thing. I want you to water the horses too. I'm not sure how long all this is going to take."

The boys both acknowledged his commands and set out to complete the task.

Abigail was pouring herself a cup of coffee when Samuel walked in. He paused in the doorway to admire his wife from behind. He removed his hat and placed it on the table by the door. He thought, after all these years of marriage, she still was the most beautiful person alive. She had put up with so much throughout the years.

Samuel worked long hours at his blacksmith shop. There was no such thing as a closing time. If one of the locals needed a blacksmith, it was usually an emergency that couldn't wait until the next morning. Samuel rarely turned down business. That meant many hours away from home. It left most of the child-rearing duties to Abigail. He was grateful she was doing such an excellent job. Other than the normal mischievous things kids do, they were all very well-mannered and respectful.

Abigail turned and saw Samuel standing in the doorway, watching her.

"Well, how long have you been there?" she asked.

Samuel gave a smile and said, "Only a few seconds. That's about how long it takes me to realize I'm the luckiest man in these parts because I have the most beautiful wife there is."

She smiled graciously at his compliments. She too felt grateful for the husband she had. He was strong and rugged, but yet he possessed a romantic quality that reminded her often that she was worth a great deal to him. He provided their family with a good living through all his hard work.

"Got time for a cup of coffee, Samuel?" she said with a hint of flirting in her voice.

"For you, my dear, anytime, anywhere" was his reply.

She poured a cup of coffee into his favorite mug. The aroma filled the air. The two of them sat at the table, drinking coffee and conversing.

"So what do you think of these boys and their ideas for the river?" she asked.

"Abigail, I don't know how we're going to get through to them about the dangers of the river. I'm just glad this fellow they found showed up. It's probably what stopped them from making the river's edge," Samuel said.

"Well, I think the punishment Tommy received will make him think twice about trying to go there again."

Abigail was confident about her answer.

The two of them continued with small talk about the day's activities. When Samuel had finished his coffee, he leaned over and kissed Abigail gently on the cheek.

"I'm sure we'll be home before dark. Time to go be neighborly to someone in need," he said.

He rose from the chair and headed for the door. He stopped before walking out, picked up his hat, turned to Abigail, and gave her a wink. She returned a smile that only Samuel recognized as *I love you too*.

The boys were already in the wagon, ready to go. They had finished spreading a layer of hay in the back so Steve would have a more comfortable ride.

They also made sure the horses were watered and the water canister was filled.

"Okay, you two youngins, time to see what you discovered," Samuel said.

He grabbed the reins to the wagon and whipped them once, which brought the horses to life. The wooden wagon groaned and creaked as it moved down the path toward the river.

As the wagon bounced along the path, Samuel had a slight smile on his face, reminiscing about himself being a little boy and his daydreams about where the end of the path was. His parents too had warned him about going to the river. However, unlike Tommy, he listened and stayed away. He was eighteen years old before he ventured to the treacherous banks of the Mississippi River.

When he was nineteen, Samuel and a group of his childhood friends decided to camp near the shore one night. One of his closest friends, Robert, went for a swim. The rest of the group sat around the camp, drinking homemade whiskey and swapping stories. No one had noticed Robert slipping into the cold waters for a refreshing dip. Almost instantly, he suffered the effects of the chilly waters and began having a difficult time staying afloat.

The currents were swift and dangerous, and as Robert slipped below the surface, the force of the river's undertow kept him pinned beneath the water. There was no way to tell how long or how far downstream the currents carried his body underwater. His clothes were found on the riverbank, but his body never was found.

Samuel remembered Robert's parents being devastated with the loss of their oldest son. From that day forward, the river had gained Samuel's respect. That day, he witnessed firsthand the unforgiving force of the river's power. The water flowed quietly past the shoreline with almost an inaudible sound, hiding its fury of what lurked below.

"Turn right, Pa!" Tommy yelled. "That's the way we went. I remember that grove of trees and that ridge. Jean is just over that ridge in a hollow," Tommy continued to instruct.

"Yep, that's the way. I remember running up that hill to get to Jean's house," Pierce chimed in.

Samuel pulled hard on the reins to turn the horses to the right toward the ridge. For most of the remaining trip, they were forging a new path. This was a route wagons did not usually go.

*　　*　　*

Jean was the first to wake from a restless night of sleep. Steve coughed and choked momentarily but remained unconscious. Jean rose from her makeshift bed and wetted Steve's lips with a canteen of water. If this man was to survive, she was going to have to get some liquids into his system. Steve again coughed as the water trickled down his parched throat. Although he wasn't coherent to anything, he could sense the touch of someone helping him.

Steve had survived the night, and Jean began thinking about where the man would stay to recuperate from his injuries. Her initial thought was of the small room on the back of the schoolhouse that contained all the essentials for living. Her cabin was just a few hundred feet from the schoolhouse. Jean knew she would be able to keep an eye on the man's healing process by having him stay there.

She had not thought of the rumors that would soon start to filter through the town folk. Instead, she thought about once he was strong enough, she would require him to work for room and board. A man's job is never done on a homestead, and since she didn't have a man, the work had piled up.

Jean stopped her mind from wandering. She realized the man may not live to see tomorrow, and if he did, once he was well enough, he most likely would leave just as mysteriously as he appeared. Jean decided to go back to living in the now.

"Over that way, Pa. Head for that ridge!" Tommy explained to his dad as he pointed in the direction of a grove of trees and underbrush.

They passed the raft that Tommy and Pierce had left beside the small trail. Samuel glanced at it but said nothing. The boys just looked at one another, fully expecting Samuel to give another tongue-lashing about the river's dangers.

They came to the top of a hollow. Steve and Jean were down below. Samuel pulled back on the reins and brought the wagon to a stop. He looked toward the bottom of the ravine. Years of erosion from water runoff had cut a deep valley. The ride down was steep.

"This is going to be a bit tricky, maneuvering down there, but it can be done."

Samuel told the two boys to hold on. With a quick whip of the reins, the horses turned and headed downhill. It was a little frightening for Tommy and Pierce. They were not accustomed to doing such wild riding in a wagon. Nevertheless, they were at home with the adventure. As the wagon bumped, groaned, and creaked down the incline, both boys were grinning from ear to ear.

Jean turned toward the commotion the horses and the wagon were making on their treacherous ride to the bottom of the ravine.

"Ah, the boys are coming," Jean mumbled.

She was relieved to see them. She turned to Steve, who was still unconscious, and said, "Well, mister, you might just make it after all."

Samuel pulled back hard on the reins when he reached the clearing where Jean was. The horses reared back and snarled at the command to stop. After a few snorts, they settled down, and Samuel and the boys climbed from the wagon to greet Jean.

"Morning, Ms. Jean," Samuel said as he tipped his hat toward her. "It looks like this guy has gotten himself into a bit of a mess."

"I would say so. I wasn't sure he would make it through the night," Jean answered.

The two boys moved closer to Steve to get a better look as Samuel and Jean talked next to the wagon. Tommy bent down to look at Steve's face. He was almost eye to eye with Steve.

"Sure looks as bad as he did last—"

Tommy suddenly stopped in midsentence, startled by what took place. There was dead silence for a moment as if the world had eerily stood still. For the first time since the plane crash, Steve opened his eyes wide. He and Tommy stared intently at one another for what seemed like an eternity. The present had met the past, eye to eye, for the first time.

"Where am I?" was all Steve could seem to muster the strength to ask.

"Pa, Ms. Jean! He's awake!"

Tommy jumped back from Steve, but the two of them had their eyes locked on one another. Something strange was happening. However, neither had any idea what.

Jean rushed to Steve.

"Mister, what's your name?"

"Steve Mitchell," he replied weakly and with a bit of puzzlement in his voice.

Steve still could not figure out what was going on. He remembered the mechanical problems he had with his plane. He remembered being hurled through the windshield, but that was about all. Now he was face-to-face with someone who was different in appearance than what he would have expected from an emergency medical team.

"Who beat you up like this?" Jean asked.

"N . . . n . . . no one," Steve managed to stammer.

"Well, how did you get so busted up?" Jean continued to ask.

"I crashed my plane" was all Steve could respond.

He felt the strength going from him. The sky went from blue to gray, and finally it went dark again. The pain had caused him to lapse into unconsciousness once again.

Jean looked at Samuel.

"I crashed my plane? Well, what does that mean?" Jean asked aloud.

"I'm not sure, but I do know with as bad as this fellow is busted up, no telling what he might say. Let's load him up and get him out of here while he's still blacked out. I don't think we have enough whiskey to drown the pain this guy would feel, riding in the back of this here wagon, if he were awake," Samuel said.

"Okay then, let's get it going," Jean replied. "He's not going to get any better lying here on the ground. We'll just head to my place for now."

Samuel bent down next to Steve's limp body. He placed his arms under Steve's back and under his legs and lifted his six-foot-two body straight up. Samuel had unbelievable strength for a man in his forties. It came from years of backbreaking blacksmith work.

He carried Steve to the wagon and lifted him up and over the side while Jean assisted in holding his broken leg. Steve gave a slight subconscious groan as his body nestled into the hay in the back of the wagon. The two boys climbed up into the back and placed a few horse blankets on him to keep him warm. Jean and Samuel climbed into the front and sat next to each other on the driver's bench.

Samuel grabbed the reins and commanded, "Giddy up!"

With a hearty snap to the leather straps, the horses sprang to life again. Samuel expertly maneuvered the wagon up the hill. Steve's limp body jiggled with the wagon's movements. Samuel was right. It was a good thing he was unconscious. The movement of Steve's broken bones back and forth would have caused unbearable pain.

Jean and Samuel sat in silence, listening to the creaking of the wooden wagon. Jean watched the trees and shrubs go by, but she really was not paying attention to any of it. Her mind was thinking of Steve again. She tried to imagine how he could have gotten into such a mess. After all, he seemed to be a very handsome and strong man. Her extraordinary ability to judge the character of people was telling her Steve was one fine person. Her thoughts of the type of man Steve was made her think of her own life.

She considered herself a desirable woman although at her age she was still single. She was to have been married by now, but life didn't work out that way. The same person who had wooed her heart had broken it. He was a fellow schoolteacher from southern Minnesota. The two of them met at a statewide social gathering for teachers.

Their initial days were spent with him chasing her romantically while she played hard to get. She finally gave in to his advances only to fall madly in love with him. They spent two years visiting each other when their schedules allowed. They wrote each other daily. A friendship blossomed into a beautiful love affair. He was a terrific writer who seemed to know what appealed to women. He kept their romantic interludes creative and fun.

Two years ago, he had left for Boston to complete some studies on governmental issues. She saw him off at the stagecoach station. As the stagecoach left and headed for the East Coast, he leaned from the window, said he would write daily, and blew her a kiss. His words did not match his actions because she never saw nor heard from him again.

Letters and telegrams went unanswered. It drove her nearly insane. Finally, after two months, she received a telegram from him saying how sorry he was and that he would not be returning to Minnesota.

She was heartbroken. It had taken her awhile to trust her heart to his promises—promises that in the end turned out to be empty. She finally came to grips with the fact that she was better off to find out now than later.

Samuel and Abigail were of great help to her during that time; the loneliness nearly paralyzed her. However, with their encouragement and watchfulness, she gradually returned to her former self. She vowed that it would be a long time before she would allow herself to be romantically involved with another man.

A large rock in the path jolted the wagon and Jean from her thoughts. She suddenly grasped at the handrails at the wagon's movements.

"Penny for your thoughts, Jean?" Samuel asked as he pulled hard on the reins to steer the horses back on the path.

"Why do you say that?" she asked.

"You seemed to be as unconscious mentally as the guy in the back is physically."

"Oh, I was just thinking of how far I have come in the last two years. This Steve guy has me thinking about it. He just seems so different. I don't know, Samuel, but there is just something intriguing about him. Maybe he just reminds me of some other guy in my past," she said with a bit of sarcasm.

Neither one had to mention his name. Samuel knew she was referring to the person who had broken her heart.

"Ms. Jean!" Tommy blurted from the back of the wagon. "I think maybe we should do something about the cut on this guy's head. It's starting to bleed again from all the bouncing he's doing back here."

Jean turned around to see blood running down Steve's head and onto the hay.

"Goodness' sakes. I should say so before the poor man bleeds to death."

Jean climbed to the back of the wagon, took a rag, wetted it with water, and applied pressure to the cut on Steve's forehead.

As she squatted on her knees, applying pressure to the cut, she stared at his facial features. She could see beyond the cuts and bruises that indeed he was a handsome man. His complexion, minus the injuries, was clear and without blemish. His blond hair was full with a bit of a wave to it. His blue eyes, as she remembered when he had them open, were the bluest she had ever seen. He looked different from all the local boys. However, what was it? She could not place her finger on it. She was really interested in this guy getting better. She had some questions she wanted to ask.

The wagon cleared a grove of trees, and Jean's schoolhouse and homestead came into view.

"Okay, mister, you've made it this far. It's all downhill from here," Jean said aloud to herself.

Samuel leaned back and asked Jean, "You gonna put him in the back room of the schoolhouse?"

"Yes, I think that would be best," Jean replied.

Samuel pulled the reins to stop the horses in front of the schoolhouse. It was a one-classroom school. Jean taught children who ranged from the age of eight to sixteen. She would get irritated that most of the children would leave to work the family farm before completing their education. Intellect was an important quality Jean looked for in people, and she wanted the kids to learn as much as they could.

Three steps on the front of the building led to a front porch that covered the entire front of the school. When the weather turned stifling, Jean would teach the class on the front porch. It was almost a toss-up to gain the children's attention on those days. If she stayed inside, the heat would distract them, and if she went outside, nature would distract them. Jean always chose the outside because at least she could be somewhat more comfortable herself.

On the back side of the school was a room that Jean used for study and storage. The room was approximately eighteen feet by twenty-five feet. It contained a fireplace, a bed in the corner, some shelving for storage, a wooden table, and a wash-basin area. She used the bed for those occasional times when children would not feel well.

Jean added a few comforts of home in the room so that on those late nights she wanted to stay and study, it would be a bit more comfortable. Somehow, studying in the school kept her motivated. She would try in her cabin, but the comforts of home would distract her from her work too easily.

Fortunately for Steve, he arrived early enough in the spring season. The kids were off school for the next three weeks. Many of the families counted on their children to help during spring-planting season.

Jean had taught at the school for ten years, and after the first year, she realized that she had better plan time off during the springtime so the children could be on the family farm. It only took one season to determine this because during her first year of teaching, only two children showed up for school, and that was because they were too young to do manual farm labor.

Samuel climbed from the wagon and went to the side where Steve was lying. Jean climbed the stairs and went into the school to prepare the bed for him. Samuel gave a grunt as he lifted Steve from the wagon. Steve was beginning to awaken from his unconscious state. As Samuel moved Steve, his broken leg hit the side of the wagon, causing Steve to cry out in agony. Jean came running from the school at the sound of Steve's yell.

"What's happening?" she asked.

"I think our friend here is beginning to feel the effects of his activities yesterday," Samuel replied.

"Bring him inside, and lay him on the bed," Jean instructed.

Tommy and Pierce jumped from the wagon and followed closely behind while Jean again assisted by holding his broken leg.

Samuel effortlessly whisked Steve's broken body up the stairs, through the schoolhouse, and to the waiting bed in the back room. Steve was becoming more aware as Samuel laid him in the bed. He knew he had survived the crash by the pain he was feeling. However, he still couldn't figure out his surroundings or the people who he was seeing. They seemed to look so old-fashioned to him.

Samuel gently laid Steve on the bed. Jean covered him with a blanket. Samuel headed for the door as Jean followed.

Near the door, Samuel turned and told her, "Jean, if you need anything, anything at all, you just ring that school bell in the yard as loud and as long as you can. Do you hear me?"

Jean smiled and jokingly said, "Okay, Pa."

She would often joke with Samuel about being *Pa* because so many times he would treat her like a daughter. Samuel did not respond except with a smirk for a smile. He knew she was joking with him.

Before walking out the door, Tommy quickly asked, "Pa, can Pierce and I stay for a bit?"

Neither wanted to miss any adventure that might be told now that it appeared Steve was becoming more conscious.

"No, I think Ms. Jean has her hands full as it is. You better come on home, and besides, young man, I think you have some firewood to stack."

Tommy looked at the floor and shuffled his feet back and forth, letting his disappointment show.

"Oh, all right," he answered in a low tone of voice.

Jean saw the disappointment in the boys and quickly said, "You know, Samuel, the man's clothes have been badly torn and shredded. Maybe you have some old clothes the boys could stop by with after a few days. All I have are old dresses, and I don't think he's my size."

The boys giggled as Samuel said with a wink, "I think I might have something he could use."

Samuel turned to walk out the door.

"Oh, and, Samuel," Jean called after him, "thank you for helping."

He paused, turned, and just smiled at her.

"Excuse me . . . but could someone tell me where I'm at?" Steve interrupted.

"Mister, I think we both have some questions to go over."

Turning back toward Samuel and the two boys, she said, "Okay, you three, git now! I've got my work cut out tending to this man's wounds."

Samuel, Tommy, and Pierce continued down the porch steps as Jean waved her hands as if she were herding goats from the room.

Jean turned back toward Steve lying in bed. She pulled a wooden chair to the edge of the bed and settled in to find out just who this person was and what happened to him out in the woods.

"So I think you said your name was . . . Steve Mitchell. Is that right?" she began.

"Yes, it is, but where am I? The last thing I remember was being thrown through the windshield of my plane." Steve spoke haltingly because of the pain he was feeling. As long as he didn't move, it was tolerable for now.

Steve couldn't help notice the puzzled look on Jean's face. She looked like he was speaking a foreign language to her.

Finally, Jean spoke up. "Mr. Steve, you just aren't making sense here. All this talk about a . . . plane and some wind thing, well, it just doesn't add up. Why don't you begin with why and who, if you can remember, beat you up."

Among the constant shots of pain, he had a puzzled, incoherent expression himself.

"Now I'm not sure what you're talking about me being beat-up. I haven't been beat up since seventh grade. I was in a plane crash. A plane, you know, one of those things that fly in the air."

Steve was feeling a bit uncomfortable with Jean's reaction and his surroundings. Although he was hurting tremendously, his concerns turned toward where he was. The conversation was leading in the direction that was as confusing to him as it was to Jean.

Jean had a more puzzled look on her face. There was a long pause of silence. Both just looked at each other, trying to decipher what the other was saying.

Steve broke the awkward silence. "Here we are in the twentieth century, and we are still facing communication barriers," he said with a bit of a smile.

Jean tried to correct him.

"You mean the nineteenth century. The twentieth century doesn't begin until the year 1900. I am a schoolteacher and—"

"Ma'am," Steve interrupted. "How about we stick with the current year of 2012? I never was much for history."

Jean thought Steve's injuries were affecting his thinking. She replied, "I hardly think the year 1863 comes even close to the year 2012! I think your injuries are making you a bit confused."

Steve paused again and took more notice of his surroundings. He then glanced at Jean dressed in a neck-to-floor dress. Her shoes, dusty and dirty, consisted of a row of buttons down each side of a leather boot. Steve was so confused.

"Did you say the year 1863?" he asked with a bit of uncertainty.

"Yes, yes, I did. Maybe you have been hit too hard and have a little loss of memory," she said with a motherly tone in her voice.

"1863? You really said 1863?" Steve questioned again.

"Why I know it is! I'm not the one who has been beat-up here. I know what's going on. I think you're the one who is a little confused," she said with confidence.

Steve remembered some rumors while in the military of the government working on a time-continuum project, but he scoffed at the idea. *Time travel is just not possible . . . or is it?* he thought. His surroundings had completely changed from the crash. He had seen four people so far that certainly were not twenty-first-century dressed. He wondered if he somehow had stumbled on the secret that the government was trying to prove. Was time travel true? Moreover, if it were, would he be stuck here? Could he ever return to the time of his family and friends? These were all questions that rapidly flooded Steve's thoughts. He thought it would be best if he just treated the situation at face value until he could solve this mystery.

"I'm sorry," Steve said. "We're getting off to a wrong start here. I have taken quite a wallop, and I'm just a little confused. I did not properly introduce myself. Hi, I'm Steve, Steve Mitchell. And your name is?"

He tried extending his hand, but that was not going to happen. Things were hurting too much. The adrenaline of the situation was wearing thin, and the pain from his injuries was beginning to surface. Even the slightest move was excruciating. He found it hard to continue concentrating.

"Well, that's much better, Mr. Mitchell. My name is Jean, and I am the schoolteacher for these parts."

"Pleased to meet you, Ms. Jean. And thank you for helping me."

"Okay, Steve, why don't you tell me what went on out there in the woods?"

Steve was not sure how to answer that question. He needed a little more time to figure out how he would explain the truth. If he truly was in the year 1863, Jean would not comprehend what Steve took for granted. In 1863, the Civil War had not ended yet, and to try to explain a complex piece of machinery like a plane would be too far-fetched for her to comprehend. Steve decided to play along for a bit.

"I'm not sure what happened out there. I know it will come to me, but for now, I guess I'm hurting a bit too much to remember it," he told her.

"Okay, I can accept that," Jean said. "Why don't you just try and relax for now. I'll heat some water and work further on cleaning up your wounds."

Jean pushed her chair back and went outside to get some firewood to place in the fireplace. Steve watched her walk out. He could see that she was a well-refined woman. When she walked, she walked with confidence.

As she disappeared out the door, he again glanced around the room. The decor certainly told him it was the year 1863. The experience was much too weird for him to understand. The shock of it all had temporarily masked over much of the pain of his injuries. Steve had momentarily accepted the fact that it was 1863 even though he couldn't understand how. He closed his eyes to try to make sense of it all. He drifted off into a deep sleep.

* * *

The roosters in the yard scattered as the wagon came to a halt in front of Samuel's cabin. The family dog yelped playfully at Tommy and Pierce as they jumped from the wagon.

"Pa, can me and Pierce play a bit before I have to stack the firewood?" Tommy asked.

"Well, I shouldn't, but I suppose you can have a little time with your friend before stacking the wood. However, not too long. You have to get that chore done. That's the price you pay for disobedience."

Tommy and Pierce dashed off toward the barn, not wanting to stick around in case Tommy's pa changed his mind. They had nothing in particular they wanted to do, but in less than a minute, they would be at the barn, and an adventure was sure to be brewing in their minds by then.

Samuel climbed the steps to his cabin. It was a modest four-room cabin. The two back rooms were added as the family grew with the birth of Tommy. Samuel and Abigail knew that the place would get smaller as the three kids grew older, but that didn't matter to them. Abigail made sure it was comfortable and kept the place in order. She was a good wife, mother, and housekeeper.

Samuel entered the kitchen where Abigail was busy preparing the evening meal. She was plucking a chicken she had recently slaughtered and was readying it to roast in the fireplace.

"So how did it go out there?" she asked Samuel.

"Well, the guy lived at least. He was really beaten badly. Jean is going to keep him in the back room at the schoolhouse."

Samuel tossed his hat on the hook next to the fireplace.

"Who is he?" Abigail asked.

"At this time, I don't know. He was out cold for most of the trip to Jean's place. He was starting to awake just as I was leaving."

"Samuel, I swear, if you don't beat all!" Abigail said with her feather-covered hands resting on her hip.

"What . . . what do you mean I beat all?" Samuel asked with a dumbfounded look on his face.

"You go to help recover a stranger, who undoubtedly was so beaten up that he was out cold, he comes to at Jean's place, and you don't bother to stick around to make sure she wouldn't need your help?"

Her voice was beginning to rise at what seemed to be her husband's unconcern for Jean's well-being. Abigail's motherly instincts were beginning to take place. As she moved her hands while talking, feathers were flying from them.

"Aw, Abigail, you're just having one of your silly woman intuitions again. Jean will be fine. There is no reason to worry about her. This guy was in no shape to be answering twenty questions or even move. Besides, if Jean needs help, all she has to do is ring the school bell, and she knows I would be right there. You had better simmer down. You're losing your feathers, and you won't be able to get off the ground," he jokingly said about the feathers flying from her hands as she talked.

He was trying to calm her emotions. Abigail turned back to the chicken she was preparing.

With a dejected tone, she said, "Well, it just doesn't seem right. A stranger we know nothing about, and who obviously has enemies out there, staying at Jean's. It just doesn't sound right, that's all."

Samuel walked up behind Abigail, put his arms around her, and gently kissed her on the neck.

"Hey, if I had a bad feeling about it, I wouldn't have left," he whispered in her ear.

Abigail could not help but smile. Samuel always seemed to be able to defuse her concerns when he wrapped his arms around her. She trusted his judgment with everything. He had a way that made her feel safe and secure when he wrapped her in his muscular arms.

*   *   *

Jean gathered as much firewood as she could carry, turned, and went back inside where Steve lay sleeping. She added the firewood to the smoldering fireplace ashes, grabbed the bellow, and began fanning the coals. Soon the crackle of a fire could be heard as the flames licked the sides of the wooden logs.

Using a ladle, Jean dipped water from the water kettle located on the lower shelf and placed it in a blackened pot. She positioned the pot so that it was over the fire. As soon as the water had heated, she filled a large wash basin. She carried the basin and a clean cloth to Steve's bedside.

She took the cloth and dipped it in the warm water, knelt next to the bed, and gently began to clean the dirt and dried blood from Steve's soiled face. His complexion beneath the grime was smooth and tanned. She repeatedly rinsed out the cloth and continued the cleaning process over his upper body. Steve lay motionless and unaware of Jean's tender touch. Each new wipe revealed how handsome he was.

It had been a long time since Jean felt that about anybody. His muscles were rigid and toned. Without removing the tattered pants he was wearing, she moved to the open area of his legs. She cleaned each one with the same tenderness. When finished, she tucked a wool blanket around his body to keep him warm. She gathered her things and paused at the door on her way out.

She looked back at Steve and thought, *He's going to make it.*

Steve continued in his unaware state as she left the room. Both were faced with questions far from being answerable. Time had dealt a blow to reality. The collision of the years 1863 and 2012 created a strange set of circumstances.

Chapter 6

Over the few following days, Steve never regained enough consciousness to hold a conversation as he did that first day in the schoolhouse. He continued in a semicomatose state. His body was reacting to his injuries by shutting down his senses. He had an awareness of someone nearby but lacked the necessary control of his motor skills to place himself in his surroundings.

Jean continued during this time taking care of him. She would often feed him a combination of water and beef broth to sustain his life. She continually talked to him as she tended to his needs even though his only response was an occasional groan.

A few days later, Steve again began to wake from his injury-induced comatose state. The awakening was as abrupt for Steve as it was for Jean.

Sunshine filtered through the window and into Steve's eyes. He opened them slightly, trying to get his bearings on where he was. It now was several days into this bizarre adventure. Before slipping into an incoherent state, Steve remembered a conversation about it being the year 1863. The surroundings he saw reminded him it wasn't a dream and that he possibly could be in the 1800s. The wooden floors, the furniture, and the structure of the building itself lent credence to the fact that he was a long way from home. He vaguely remembered anything of the last several days.

The door opened, and a sweet aroma of bacon filled the room. Jean, looking freshly cleaned and dressed, was standing there. The smell of food was mouthwatering to Steve. He had nothing solid to eat during the last several days.

"That sure smells good," he said to Jean.

"Oh my goodness, my hunch yesterday was correct. I suspected you were waking from your incoherent state and thought you could use a little heartier food. If you still hadn't fully recovered consciously, I was going to have to eat all this food myself. I have to tell you I have a lot of questions to ask. For the last several days, I have been the one doing all the talking. I wasn't sure if you would ever wake up. You must be hungry for something more than beef broth by now," she said to Steve.

Jean set the pot of food she was carrying on the table.

"How's the soreness?" she asked.

"Oh, I'm pretty sore. In fact, it downright hurts," Steve answered.

"The two boys who found you are bringing some clothes for you later on," Jean continued. "I think what you're wearing is pretty much ready to be burned. I brought something else for you, but I'm not sure you can use them yet."

She went back outside and carried in two handcrafted crutches for Steve. Last year, one of the bigger kids in her school was up to horseplay and fell from a tree. His father made the crutches so his son could get back and forth to school. The father was not about to let him miss his schooling. After the leg healed, he never took them back home and left them at the school.

Walking over to Steve's bedside, she held out the crutches.

"I figured you must be feeling a little uncomfortable by now. Just so you know, the outhouse is out the door and to the right. However, you are on your own there. That's where I draw the line on helping," Jean said, smiling.

"No problem," Steve answered back. "I have to learn to do things for myself again, don't I?"

Jean leaned the crutches up against the bed and helped Steve sit up. He sat there a bit to let his body adjust to the new position. After a few moments, Jean helped him to a standing position with the aid of the crutches. He stood there a moment, leaning on them. It felt good to be in an upright position, but he was very dizzy and winced at the pain. It felt like an eternity since he had stood up. Of course, he favored the left crutch. His right arm still hurt too much to put much pressure on it.

"Well, this is a start," he told Jean. "Now which way is that outhouse?"

Jean reminded him, "Out the door and to your right. You can't miss it. Why don't you go take care of your business, and I'll get your breakfast ready."

Jean began placing the breakfast food she had brought on the table while Steve moved slowly across the floor on his crutches. Once outside, he looked around at the surroundings. How beautiful it was. There were trees everywhere. Steve listened to the birds as they sang back and forth. He heard the wind gently rustle the tree leaves. How odd it was not to hear any modern conveniences such as a distant jet or automobile. The air was so clean and fresh. Only the smell of Jean's bacon wafted through it.

Steve thought about how much he enjoyed the outdoors. He concentrated hard on manipulating the crutches so that he wouldn't take a tumble and break something else. With his right side being so busted up, it hurt to put too much weight on it.

Steve returned to his temporary living quarters after a much-labored visit to the outdoor latrine. He had not used one quite like that since childhood. It brought back memories of a simpler time in his life.

Jean was sitting at the table with breakfast for the two of them already set out when he returned.

"My goodness, Jean, that smells great!"

"Well, it should. When was the last time you ate a hot meal?" she asked Steve.

"Let me see, I guess it was a burger and fries, but I can't remember how long ago."

"A what?" Jean asked with confusion in her voice.

"Oh yeah, I guess fast-food restaurants haven't been invented yet."

Jean still looked puzzled. Steve realized that a slip of the future could cause him major problems if he wasn't careful. He needed to explain his dilemma carefully but not too quickly. He was not quite sure if Jean would grasp the severity of the situation.

Steve hobbled over to the table and sat down. He was in constant pain from his injuries. The wooden plates and wooden utensils Jean had set out were new to him. It was like eating with salad-bowl utensils.

"Would you like a cup of coffee?" Jean asked Steve.

"Sure. I feel as though I hadn't had one for some time. I could use one," he replied.

Jean walked to the fireplace where she had placed a kettle of coffee over the fire while Steve was outside. She took a mug from the fireplace mantle and poured the dark liquid from the kettle into it. The aroma told Steve that this was going to be a strong cup of coffee. She placed the mug on the table in front of him, returned to her chair, and continued eating.

Steve thought about asking for cream and sugar but refrained. He didn't think she would have it. In the 1860s, if you wanted coffee, you got coffee, and that was it. Steve sipped slowly on the mug, trying to stomach the strong taste.

Jean took a sip of coffee and nonchalantly asked Steve, "So have you gained any of your memory yet about how you got so beat-up?"

Steve hesitated to answer, not knowing what to say.

"Well?" Jean asked again.

"Yeah, I guess it's clear to me what happened. But before I tell you, can I ask some questions about you?"

Steve tried to be as sincere as possible about asking Jean any questions.

"Hey, I'm not the outsider here. So why should I be the one to answer questions?" she replied. She was confused why this stranger would start to question her. Jean was a very independent woman and didn't want to have to answer to anyone, let alone a stranger.

"Please?" Steve responded.

With a puzzled voice, Jean answered, "I just don't understand what you need to ask me, but go ahead if you must."

Steve said thank you and then went about trying to determine how he was going to explain to Jean that he actually lived almost 150 years later than she lived. It was a difficult task to do, difficult because Steve had to convince not only Jean but himself as well. He decided to start by finding out how open she was to thinking outside the box.

"Jean, being a teacher, do you think about what's out there?"

"Out there? What do you mean, '*Out there*'?"

Steve continued, "I mean, do you ever think of what's really out there? Out there beyond our own air we breathe?"

Sarcastically she replied, "Yeah, the sun, the moon, the stars, the planets. What is it you are trying to ask? Remember that I am a teacher. I've studied the sun, the moon, and the stars."

"I know, I know. Nevertheless, have you thought about the things you can't explain out there? Like how does the moon stay in place? How can the sun keep shining? I believe God put them there, but how did he do it? What method did he use to make the universe?"

Jean now understood the type of questions he was asking. His questions had a philosophical flair to them. She had a bit of understanding with her answer.

"Why, sure, I think of those things. I believe there are things in this world that I'll never understand. I believe that's God's plan for our lives. Each generation learns new and better ways of doing things. We have so much more now than the Pilgrims had when they first came to America. I think the next generation will have much more than what *this* generation has. If our generation knew everything, what would the kids of today have to look forward to? There would be no new things to discover. There would be a lack of motivation to learn. People, as well as this country, would eventually cease to exist in short order."

After Jean's answer, Steve was confident he could get her to understand where he came from. He took another sip of coffee, tried to change his position in his chair, which caused him a great deal of discomfort, and continued his attempt to explain.

"Jean, you have a wonderful view of life. I too believe each generation learns, creates, establishes, or whatever, a new and better life than the generation before. Now I want you to really think. Don't think of the next generation, but think of three, four, or maybe even five generations from now. What changes could you expect in the way we live and work?"

Jean paused and stared at Steve while thinking about his thought-provoking questions. She thought they were some odd questions to be asking.

"Steve, I can't think of anything. I am sure that things will be totally different, but I don't know how. I can't even imagine it."

Steve knew that it was now or never to tell her of himself. He wasn't sure how she was going to react. He felt as though he were dreaming everything. Finally, the best way he knew to describe himself was to be blunt.

"Jean, you asked about who beat me up. Well, no one did. I come from a long time in the future. I crashed my plane, which is a machine man uses to fly from one point to the other. I don't know how it happened. I can't explain it. I don't even know what happened to the wreckage. One minute I'm flying in the year 2012, and within seconds I wake up in the year 1863. I tell you it doesn't make sense, but it happened."

Jean dropped her fork and stared intently at Steve. The first instincts going through her mind was that Steve was a crazy man. How absurd of him to think he came from another generation. How absurd to think she would believe him. Who was he trying to kid? After a long pause, Jean finally spoke up.

"Evidently, you still are disoriented from your injuries. I think you better lie down and get some more rest," she indignantly told him.

"Jean . . . Jean, it's *true!*"

Steve reached out to touch her hand.

She immediately pulled it back and said, "No, I think you need some more rest."

She stood and began quickly clearing the breakfast from the table. Steve sighed at her rebuff.

"You have to believe me. I think you are my only hope of returning to my generation. Anyone else would have strung me up from the nearest tree by now. I feel I can trust you. You yourself said you believed other generations in the future would know more. Maybe I came from one of those generations. Maybe they figured out a way for time travel. I don't know. You and I can no easier explain how this happened than we can explain how God created the elements that make up our universe."

Jean was so confused. On one hand, Steve made sense; on the other, he talked crazy. She looked at him and saw the sincerity in his blue eyes. She heard a pleading for help and a pleading for a little understanding in his voice. She had nothing to say right now. All she wanted to do was to leave and gather her thoughts.

"I don't want to hear such madness!" she said as she bolted out the door and into the school courtyard.

Steve tried to go after her, but the pain in his body was too great. Instead, he could only manage to hobble over to the bed and sit down, expecting the worst. He imagined Jean telling the town folk that he was crazy. He imagined they would soon come and run him off or, worse yet, kill him for such blasphemy.

Meanwhile, Jean leaned against the pole that held the school bell. She thought about what Samuel had said about ringing the bell if she needed help. She was certain Steve was a maniac, which made her afraid for her life. She rationalized the situation before she grabbed the rope to start ringing the bell. He was too weak to come after her. He certainly had some knocks to the head. Nevertheless, he talked and acted with sincerity.

Then she thought about what she said regarding her generation being much better than the Pilgrims' generation. She thought about the change that had taken place. What if the tables were turned and she went back in time and sat with the Pilgrims? How would she react?

"Oh, this is just ridiculous to be thinking this way. He's just crazy in the head, that's all!"

Jean firmly grasped the rope to ring the bell, but on the first tug, the rope went limp and fell down around her feet. It had come loose from the bell housing. Jean couldn't ring the bell now until she got the ladder out and retied the rope. This delay caused her to have second thoughts about what she just heard.

She reasoned, if he was right, it is a wonderful bit of knowledge, and no telling what would happen to him if the town folk got wind of this.

Jean found herself wandering back to the schoolhouse. Once inside, she looked at Steve sitting uncomfortably on the edge of the bed. He had an appearance to him that was different from the rest of the local men. Because of the condition of his clothes, or lack mostly thereof, she could see his muscular body. It had a different appearance to it than the men around town. The muscles were toned in a different fashion. She doubted that he ever manhandled a plow behind a pair of oxen. It was almost like his body was conditioned under another form of physical exercise.

Steve groaned at the pain as he lay back down.

"I'm not crazy, Jean. What I told you is true."

Jean was confused and didn't know what to say. Finally, she walked toward the bed. As she passed the table, she reached out and grabbed a chair to drag along behind her. She got to the edge of the bed, placed the chair directly in front of Steve, sat down, and stared at him for a moment.

Steve didn't say anything. He just stared back at her. Finally, she spoke up.

"I don't know what to say. I only know you as an injured man that was found in the woods. I give you a place to heal. I feed you, and all of a sudden, you blurt that you are from some time in the future. You talk about some flying contraption. What am I supposed to think? You seem normal in every way, but then you talk like a lunatic. How do you expect me to believe such nonsense?"

Steve turned away from Jean and rested his good arm across his forehead.

"Jean, I understand you're confused. I would react the same way. However, look at me. I'm all busted up. If I was a madman and had some crazy notion in my mind, do you think I would tell you such things, knowing I couldn't get up and run away?"

Steve spoke with sincerity.

"What I told you is the truth. I live in the year 2012 with so many exciting inventions that haven't even been thought of yet by the people of your time. I can't explain it any more than you can believe it. However, here we are, two people from two different times, facing each other. What are we going to do?"

There was a pause as the two of them pondered the circumstance. Steve lowered his arm from his forehead and turned back to Jean.

"Why don't we try to accept this at face value? I'll believe I am living in 1863, and you believe I came from the future. I don't want to be here any more than you want me here."

Steve hesitated and retraced his thoughts.

"I mean, here in the year 1863, not here as far as you helping me. I am very grateful for all you have done so far."

Jean didn't say anything. She stood up and dragged the wooden chair back to its place by the table. She paused while standing there, leaning on the chair.

After a short time, she regained her upright posture and simply said, "Okay."

She couldn't believe she was accepting his story. Nevertheless, she was audacious and always accepted things at face value.

Steve felt relieved and said, "Okay, I guess this is the first step in trying to find out how this happened and, even more importantly, if it will ever go back to normal."

Jean answered, "This is so far removed from reality, and if I find out you're lying, well, God help you. I will not be made into a fool."

Steve answered her, "I can assure you that you won't come out looking like a fool. I'll be very protective of that."

Jean gathered her things and turned to leave the room. Steve watched as she walked away. She moved with grace and dignity. He was impressed with her stature and kindness.

"Jean, thank you," Steve called after her with sincerity.

She turned back to him from the door and repeated, "I will not be made into a fool."

With that, she left the room.

Steve closed his eyes and tried to concentrate on what could have happened. How could he have ended up in 1863? Where was his plane? What about the mysterious crate he was to deliver in a few days? Could it have had something to do with this? The thought of it all was causing a massive headache. His injuries were painful enough. Soon he was able to drift off to sleep, which temporally masked the pain.

Jean returned to her cabin and began cleaning up from preparing the morning meal. She still was having a hard time understanding herself. Face value in her mind, Steve was a maniac. However, there was something about him that left her so intrigued. He was so different from anyone she knew. He spoke elegantly. He seemed to be well educated. He certainly was a mystery to her.

Jean finished cleaning up and went to her desk. Since her fiancé undoubtedly ran off with another woman, she kept a diary of her life. Writing helped her express her emotions. It provided a form of therapy for the pain she was going through at the time. She continued to write although her emotions of the situation had subsided somewhat. Today's entry was certain to be a long one. There was so much to tell. After all, not every day does someone from the future come waltzing into your life!

Jean reached for her diary that was under a stack of essay assignments she previously had the children do. She had assigned them to write a single-paragraph essay about if they had the ability to do anything, what would they do. Tommy's happened to be on the top. His title caught her eye. "Flying Like a Bird."

She pulled the essay and read it again. However, this time she read it not with the intent to grade but for the subject content, especially after what she had just experienced. The essay read,

> I wish I could fly like a bird. That way I could go where I want. I would go places I have never seen before. I could visit faraway places and see new things. I would fly to the moon.

As Jean read the simple writing of the eleven-year-old boy, she thought of what Steve had said about flying. If it really was true that he was from the future, does that mean the years of imagination actually produced reality?

She decided she had to stop trying to rationalize what Steve had told her. She planned to take one day at a time.

* * *

It was several days before Tommy finished stacking the firewood. It was a tough job. It could have been done much quicker, but Tommy would too often be sidetracked with his imagination.

Pierce came over shortly after lunch and helped finish the pile. As the two boys worked side by side, the topic of their conversation turned toward Steve.

"Do you think he'll leave soon?" Pierce asked Tommy.

"I don't know. Ms. Jean has taken good care of him," Tommy replied as he placed a split log on the top of the pile.

"He sure was beat-up bad. I wonder what he did," Pierce questioned aloud.

Tommy didn't answer. He was trying to think of what could have happened himself. The vivid imaginations of the two eleven-year-olds were starting to take over.

"Maybe he was a bank robber, and his partners beat him up?" Tommy said with a questioning voice.

"Yeah, maybe they just robbed a bank, and they didn't want to split the loot with him."

"I don't know," Tommy replied. "I would think they'd try to kill him."

"Maybe they lost their guns," Pierce tried to reason.

Tommy thought a minute and said, "Or maybe they wanted to teach him a lesson, and he blacked out on them. Either way, the man was beat-up bad. Let's hurry up and stack this wood so we can get on over to the schoolhouse and ask him ourselves."

"I hope he's awake today," Pierce said.

The boys finished stacking the wood and went inside Tommy's cabin to grab the old clothes Samuel was sending for Steve and took off without even the slightest hesitation. They wanted to find out who this person was. Their childhood imaginations were running wild.

The boys raced down the path to Jean's cabin. As they came into the clearing, they stopped to discuss where to go. They questioned whether to go straight to the schoolhouse or stop by Jean's cabin. They decided to see her first because there was a question in their minds whether Steve was conscious or not.

Jean finished making an entry in her diary about the day's events. She wrote what she felt. She was having a hard time understanding why her intellect even questioned the man's story. Nevertheless, she couldn't help believing there was something to it. She closed the diary and was resting her hands on it when she heard someone knocking on the door.

"Ms. Jean, are you here?"

Immediately she recognized the voices of Tommy and Pierce. She placed her diary in her desk drawer while wondering what she would tell the boys. She knew they would be full of questions.

"Yes, boys, I'm here. Come on in."

Both rushed in eager to hear any news about Steve.

"Good morning, Ms. Jean," both boys cordially said.

The two boys' parents had done a great job teaching their kids to respect others.

"How's Steve?" Tommy asked.

"I'm happy to tell you two that he is very much alive and talking. You two should be proud of yourselves for being alert to helping him. I don't think he would have survived much longer if it weren't for you two coming along. I took him breakfast earlier, and right now, I believe he is resting."

The boys could hardly wait to find out what happened.

"Did he tell you who beat him up?" Pierce asked.

Jean paused while looking at the boys. She questioned whether to tell them the truth or make up a story. She looked into the eager eyes of the two boys, and she could see their desire to learn. Jean couldn't bring herself to lie to such innocence.

"Boys, why don't you sit down at the table, and let me get you some snacks."

She needed a little time to formulate the right words to tell them. She brought a plate of oatmeal cookies she had baked the day before. She placed the plate between the boys and sat down across from them.

"Boys, maybe I should, and then again maybe I shouldn't, but I am going to tell you the truth about what Steve told me. He told me something that, as an adult, I have a hard time believing."

Jean had concluded that the two boys could easier understand what she was about to say because their minds were those of a child, sweet and innocent and without the adult tendencies to judge.

Jean began, "I want you to listen carefully to what I have to say. Steve is different from us. He comes from a faraway place, a place that is probably only in your imagination."

Tommy looked at her with a puzzled look and said, "Huh?"

Jean thought about what she had said, and it confused her. She had to make it simpler, so she told them like it was.

"Steve claims he is from the year 2012. He said he had some sort of contraption that allowed him to fly like the birds. During a storm, it somehow smashed to the ground, and he woke up some 150 years in the past with us."

The boys' eyes were wide-open at this point. Jean could see that their imaginations had accepted the information as nothing but the truth. There was no question of how or why. They were just astonished. The thought of being from the future never even crossed their minds. They just looked at each other in amazement.

Finally, Tommy let out a long, sustained, hushed tone, simply saying, "Wow!"

"Can we go see him?" Pierce excitedly asked.

Jean thought for a moment.

"I suppose I should go check on him. It's been a couple of hours since I saw him last. I should make sure he's okay."

The two boys were up and racing out the door almost before she got the words out.

"Hold on, you two," she called after them. "Don't forget these clothes you brought for him, and remember, he is a sick man, and we're not going to barge in on him like a stampede of buffalo. You boys just follow me."

The three of them walked across the common area between Jean's place and the schoolhouse. She was a bit amazed at how she was feeling. She was now starting to accept Steve's story as truth.

With a slight smirk on her face and under her breath, she simply told herself, "Hmmm, interesting."

Jean climbed the short steps to the schoolhouse with the two boys closely in tow. Now that she was more inclined to believe Steve's story about being from the future, she felt a sense of excitement. Like the boys, she wanted to know more.

The three gently entered the room so as not to disturb Steve if he was sleeping. Surprisingly, she found him sitting at the table, thumbing through one of the schoolbooks in the room.

"Jean, this is fascinating to look at—"

He stopped abruptly when he saw the two boys behind her.

"I remember you guys," Steve said. "Weren't you two the ones who found me out in the woods?"

"Yes, sir," Tommy replied.

"Well, I can't thank you enough. I still am pretty busted up, but with Jean's help, I'm able to move around a little more," Steve told the boys.

Pierce couldn't take the suspense any longer.

"Mister, how can you fly like a bird?" he asked outright.

Steve had a surprised look on his face. He was unprepared for the question.

"Uh, boys, could I have a word alone with Ms. Jean for a minute?"

Tommy and Pierce looked at Jean for approval.

"It's okay, boys. Would you two do me a favor? Set those clothes on the bed, go to the woodshed, and bring an armload of firewood in here."

Both boys agreed. They tossed the clothes on the bed in no special order as you might expect boys to do and raced out the door.

Jean turned from watching the two boys leave and said to Steve, "Yes, what is it?"

"Uh, Jean . . . did you tell the boys what I told you?" he asked her.

Jean was feeling a bit uncomfortable with the tone in his voice. She didn't like to be questioned.

"Yes, yes, I did. I don't make it a habit not to tell the truth, especially to children," she indignantly replied.

Steve sighed and said, "I wish you hadn't done that. We have yet to figure out between the two of us how in the world this happened, and you go tell someone else?"

Jean looked Steve in the eye and sternly said, "Well, excuse me, sir! I am not the one to be questioned here. I'm the one who lives here, remember?"

"Yes, I know, but do you understand the implications here? I've studied your time era in college, and if some people think I'm a madman, it could get dangerous for both of us."

Steve realized from the expression on Jean's face that arguing the fact was not going to solve the situation. He changed his tone from confrontation to finding a solution.

"Okay, okay. I know I have told you some strange things here, and I am thankful it appears that you now believe me, but we need to be careful with this information. I too am not one to tell lies, so we're going to have to get the kids to understand that this information must be kept quiet for the good of all of us."

Jean too was backing down from her sudden confrontational attitude.

"I suppose you're right. I think the boys can keep it quiet if we join them into trying to figure out what happened."

Jean couldn't believe what she was saying. She in essence agreed to the validity of Steve's story.

She pondered the thought and said, "Well, Mr. Mitchell, I hope you like mysteries because we certainly have a real live one here."

Steve chuckled. "I do like a good mystery, but I am not accustomed to it surrounding me."

Tommy and Pierce both returned to the room in the schoolhouse with an armload of firewood.

"Here ya go, Ms. Jean."

Jean thanked the boys and instructed them to place it by the fireplace. She then had them sit down with her and Steve at the table so Steve could relate his story. The two of them had a big job ahead: to involve the imagination of the two boys and yet keep it quiet from the rest of the town folks.

Chapter 7

Samuel was busy repairing a wagon wheel when Leroy, Jacob, and Jack entered Samuel's blacksmith shop. All three were in their early thirties. They were just a little too old to join the Civil War, which was happening at the time, not that the three would contribute even if they could! The three had nothing constructive to do except discuss the arrival of a stranger to the area. All three worked as part-time farmhands at various homesteads around the area.

In town, everyone knew everyone else's business, and Steve's arrival at the schoolhouse was big news. Nothing escaped the local grapevine of information. Without television or radio, people communicated much more on a one-on-one basis than what people of the twenty-first century do.

Leroy, a tall thin man with a balding scalp, was the one who suggested to Jacob and Jack about going to see Samuel. He thought Samuel would have the latest hearsay of the new stranger in town because he had talked to him the morning Samuel left with the wagon to pick Steve up. Jack, clearly the strongest of the three with his muscular six-foot-three-inch body, agreed with a smile on his face. Jacob was the quietest of the bunch. He was the most responsible of the group, but he wasn't a saint. Often his efforts kept the other two from serious trouble. Most of the time, they just made a nuisance of themselves at the local saloon.

Samuel looked up from his work to see the group of men walk in. He laid his tools down and wiped his hands on the soiled leather apron he was wearing.

"Well, this looks like trouble," Samuel jokingly said.

"Why, Samuel, you know when the three of us get together, we're doing nothing but solving this country's problems," Leroy joked back.

"Actually, we're here to talk to you about this guy staying over at Jean's place," Jacob told Samuel.

Samuel ignored the comment, turned, picked up his hammer, and began banging on the wagon wheel again. Samuel's temper inside began to flare. He knew the three were there to try to start rumors, and that was nothing Samuel was going to have a part of. He despised rumors and gossip.

After a few hits, he stopped, walked over to Leroy, looked him in the eye, and sternly said, "Leroy, do you think I'm stupid? I know what you want me to do. You want me to start telling you about this guy so the three of you can go about town using my words to stir up the town folk. It ain't gonna happen! Do you hear me? It just ain't gonna happen! I helped Jean with this guy because he was a fellow human being who was hurt badly. With all the death and destruction this blasted north-and-south conflict has brought our way, it felt good to help someone on the road to recovery rather than put a gun to someone's head and blow him away!"

Samuel seethed with anger at the actions of the three idiots who stood before him. The three thugs realized they had crossed the line with Samuel and tried to diffuse the situation.

"Okay, okay, you don't have to get riled up, Samuel," Leroy said smoothly. "Just simmer down. We're not here to cause trouble. Uh . . . uh, the three of us were headed for the saloon for a drink. Do you want to come?"

Leroy was looking for an excuse to leave and leave quickly. They had not bargained for Samuel's angry outburst.

"No, I have work to do," Samuel sternly replied and went back to the wagon wheel he was working on.

The three troublemakers left hurriedly out the door they came in. Once outside, Leroy lit up a half-used cigar to calm his nerves as they strolled toward the saloon. All three were just a bit shaken by Samuel's angry outburst.

"What do you suppose set him off like that?" Leroy asked the other two.

"If you ask me, he's hiding something about this guy. That's not the Sam we know. Something's up." Jack was convinced of it.

Secretly, each was just a little disturbed about some guy hanging around Jean. All three had previously made advances toward her, and each time, they came away rebuffed. Jean was much classier than the three, and they knew it. However, that still didn't stop the frequent attempts to try to take her to the local dances. The three goons continued slowly toward the saloon, puffing on cigars and poking fun at Steve, a man they knew nothing about.

* * *

Steve saw the amazement on the boys' faces as he described the events that brought him to the year 1863. Even Jean had a look of astonishment as she listened for the second time to the story. The boys had no problem accepting Steve's explanation of what happened to him. Their young lives hadn't experienced all that life had to offer, affording them the ability to believe what their imagination wanted.

"Now, Tommy and Pierce, we were discussing that we need your help to solve how I got here and how I am going to get back. I have told you a lot so far, and it is important that you keep this between the four of us. Some of the town folk might want to send me away or maybe harm me because they would see me as a threat. Do you understand?"

Tommy and Pierce both agreed. Then Tommy had a perplexed look on his face.

"What if my folks ask me about you? I can't lie to them. That would get me in a lot of trouble."

Jean looked at Steve, and she knew Tommy was right.

"I'll tell you what. I'll talk to your parents," Steve replied.

Jean could see that the pain was getting worse for Steve. The stiff chair offered little in the way of comfort.

"Boys, I think we better let Steve get some rest now. He's still really sore from his ordeal and needs to lie down. Both of you can come back tomorrow."

Both boys stood to go, but before leaving, Tommy asked Steve, "What was the name of that machine you said flew like a bird?"

"A plane, Tommy. An airplane."

"Hmmm, sure wish I had one," Tommy replied.

After the boys left, Jean and Steve continued talking about their discussion with the boys.

"You know the boys better than I. Do you think they'll keep quiet?" Steve asked Jean.

"I don't know. I really don't know. This has been so much to take in, and I am not sure their little minds can keep it there. We'll just have to wait and see."

"Jean, do you believe me now?"

Jean gave a sigh and said, "I don't know what's crazier: your story or me believing it. Yes, in a strange way, I do believe it, but there is one thing

I want you to promise." Jean leaned forward and looked straight into Steve's blue eyes as she said, "I am not promised tomorrow or even the next hour, but as long as I live, I have anticipation about my tomorrows and their unknowns. Please don't tell me how the events of my time turn out. That would take the joy out of my life. I want to experience life. I don't want life to become a textbook for me. Let me write my own chapters, please?"

Steve saw the sincerity in her eyes. He was impressed with her desire for life. If she wanted, she could have everything by just knowing what the future holds, but her joy was not found in the things this world had to offer. It was found in learning and experiencing the changes of the season of life. Her attitude was very attractive to him.

"Jean, I have lived a life that, so far, has been tremendously fulfilling because I accomplished it on a day-to-day basis. If it were handed to me on a silver platter, it wouldn't mean as much to me. What means everything to me is the people who have helped me become who I am. You are so right. Life is a mystery, and to live it to its fullest, you have to take one day at a time. I would be devastated if I took that from you. I can see you are a wonderful person. You didn't *have* to help me, but you *chose* to help me. I can't thank you enough."

Jean felt the tear in her eye. It had been a long time since someone complimented her like that. It felt good to her. She knew she was a good person, and she admired Steve for recognizing that.

"Thank you, Steve. Why don't you lie down and get some rest? I'll bring you something to eat later on."

Steve thanked her and hobbled to the bed. She walked out the door, and each felt a keen sense of caring.

* * *

Steve wasn't sure what time it was when he woke up. The sun was fairly low in the western horizon. He remained in bed, gathering his thoughts. How he missed his parents. He wondered if he would ever see them again. Would he ever experience the modern conveniences of home again? Steve fought the depression the thoughts brought to him. One thing life had taught him was to make the best of the situation at hand.

His sense of smell caught the scent of his body odor, and he knew he had better make use of the water in the corner if he expected Jean to visit him with dinner.

With no modern zippers or snaps to work with, he struggled to get out of the clothes he was wearing. He shuffled to the water canister, took a cloth, and dipped it in the water. His body shivered as the cold water touched his skin. He found a liquid on the shelf that smelled like soap. He cleansed himself the best he could with his limited range of motion. The whole time he was bathing, he wondered if Jean would walk in and catch him standing there with nothing on but the splints holding his broken bones in place.

The sponge bath made him feel a lot better. In addition, he now smelled tolerable. He struggled with dressing himself as much as he did undressing but accomplished it all before Jean showed up.

A few minutes after he finished, Jean walked in, carrying a pot of beef stew and a plate of fresh-baked bread. He was extremely hungry.

"I'm glad you're awake, Steve. I came earlier in the day, but you seemed to be sleeping well, and I didn't want to awaken you. If you were still sleeping this evening, I would have woken you because you need nourishment to get healthy," Jean told him.

She set the pot on the table and scooped out a huge ladleful of the creamy combination of beef and vegetables for him. Steve's smile told her how good it was.

As they ate, Steve continued to tell Jean of his former "future" life. She was fascinated by his stories. All this was so foreign to her. She continually asked questions. He was careful not to reveal too much about the future as they had previously discussed.

Steve too was interested in hearing the local news of the town folks. He had studied the Civil War era in the past, but nothing was as detailed as what Jean was telling him. Instead of facts and figures, he was getting to understand the feelings of the people behind the scenes. Both were getting firsthand knowledge that neither could find in a textbook.

After about an hour of conversation and eating, Jean finally said, "Steve, this has all been so unbelievable to me. All sane judgment says I should not even entertain such things, but I find myself being drawn closer to them. You have an amazing story. This may sound terrible, but I hope you stay. It would be a shame if you returned to where you came from."

Steve laughingly answered, "Return? I don't even know how I *got* here, so there is no way I know how to go back to my time."

Both had a chuckle at Steve's predicament.

Jean placed a couple of logs in the fireplace.

"There. That should keep you warm tonight," she said to Steve as she wiped her hands on her apron.

She gathered her things and headed for the door.

Before walking out, she turned and told Steve, "I had a great time tonight. It was nice to talk with someone."

Steve told her she was a comfort to him in a strange world. He thanked her for dinner and watched her walk out the door, noticing how gracefully she walked.

*   *   *

Steve was napping comfortably on the bed. On the edge of his consciousness, he could sense someone standing near him. He forced his eyes open to see Tommy and Pierce hovering over him and staring.

"Well, good morning, boys," Steve muttered to the two of them.

Both boys returned the greeting.

"Are you feeling better?" Tommy asked.

"Yes, I'm regaining my strength little by little, and I'm starting to move around a bit more," Steve replied.

The boys were hoping to hear more about the flying stories Steve had told them about the day before. They were young enough to not be able to distinguish between fact and fiction. It was all an adventure to them whether there was any truth to them or not.

"Steve, can you please tell us about this airplane you were talking about?"

Pierce joined Tommy in saying, "We're still not sure what that is."

Steve could see how the minds of the two were working. The gypsies talked about rafting the river, and the boys latched on to that because it was new to them. Now the concept of an airplane had their wheels turning again.

Steve thought for a moment and said, "I'll tell you what, boys. If you get me something to write on, I'll draw you a picture."

Steve knew it would be easier for them to understand the concept by seeing a picture on paper rather than trying to explain it to them.

The two boys went to the shelf on the other side of the room that held a small amount of school supplies. Steve reached for his crutches and pulled himself up to get to the table. He sat down and picked up the pencil. He was fortunate he could still write because he was left-handed. Being right-handed would have been a problem because of the condition of his right arm.

He carefully drew the picture. Steve was definitely a perfectionist, and it was necessary to have the wings, engines, and fuselage proportionate to one another. The boys were fascinated, watching Steve transfer what the boys called dreams to paper.

Steve explained each part as he drew it. He tried not to be too technical so the boys could understand it better. He drew a cylindrical form on the paper.

"First," Steve said, "this is what is called a fuselage. It holds all your belongings, and up here," Steve pointed to the front of the shape, "is where the pilot sits."

"What's a pilot?" Tommy asked.

"A pilot is the person who flies the airplane," Steve replied. "He's the one who controls whether the plane goes up, down, left, or right."

Steve was finding this conversation invigorating. After all, he was talking with two boys who had never seen or even heard of an airplane. Their minds were so impressionable. Next, he drew the wings and the rear stabilizer. He also drew two propeller engines on each wing.

"Now here is how the plane goes up in the sky."

Pointing to the two engines, Steve started to explain, "These are called engines, and when they are turned on, they spin these propellers you see on the end of the engines. When the propellers are spinning fast enough, they push air backward over the wings. Do you know what a windmill looks like that pumps water from the ground?" Steve asked the two boys.

They both were familiar with them because this was how they got their water.

Steve continued, "Unlike the windmill, where the wind moves the propellers to turn the pump, the propellers on a plane pull the air by being driven fast by the engine. This forces the wind over the wings."

This was a bit tricky for Steve to try to explain to a couple of eleven-year-olds who had no concept of future machinery. He continued anyway. He pointed out the shape of the wing and explained how the wind going over the top of the wing created a lifting effect underneath, causing the plane to rise in the air.

By now, Tommy and Pierce were fascinated by Steve's drawing but still had no clue as to Steve's feeble attempt to explain how an airplane works. He had a hard time trying not to be too technical.

"Anyway, boys, that's what an airplane looks like. And they can fly anywhere in the world."

"Wow, Steve, that sure sounds like some sort of contraption. I wish I could ride in one of those," Tommy said.

"Live long enough, and who knows," Steve replied.

The two boys could hear Jean yelling for them outside.

"We got to go," Pierce said. "Ms. Jean is going to give us each a nickel for helping her with chores today."

Steve chuckled as the two raced for the door.

"Don't spend that nickel all in one place," Steve told the boys.

When Tommy reached the doorway, he stopped and turned back and asked Steve, "Can I please have the picture you drew?"

"Why of course you can, and I'll even be a good artist and sign it for you."

Steve picked up the pencil and signed his name. "To Tommy! Steve Mitchell, May 1863." He got a kick out of doing that. Tommy folded up the autographed picture, placed it in his back pocket, and then disappeared out the door. Steve, in the meantime, turned and hobbled to the basin of water to clean up.

The boys raced across the school's common area to Jean's cabin.

"We're here, Ms. Jean. All set to help out," Pierce said.

"Okay, great. Here is what I have for you two to do. I would like you to weed the vegetable garden and restack the firewood by my door. Can you guys handle that?"

"Sure can! Oh, and by the way, Ms. Jean, my ma and pa are coming by later this morning. They told me to tell you that they want to talk with you," Tommy told Jean.

"Thanks, Tommy."

Jean walked over to see how Steve was doing. Steve smiled when she appeared in the door, enjoying the friendship that had developed.

"How are you doing today?" she asked.

"I think I'm getting better. Each day it's easier to get up."

"Samuel and Abigail are coming today," she said. "Tommy told me they would like to talk to me. I'm sure they want to find out how you got so beat-up."

Steve sat by the fireplace with a worried look on his face. Jean walked to the table and sat down. There was a pause in the conversation as the two of them thought about the situation.

"I didn't think they would wait too long to start asking," she said. "That's okay, though. Hopefully, they will have an open mind."

Jean explained to him that they were probably the closest friends she had in town. Samuel watched over her like a daughter.

The pounding of horse hoofs could be heard coming up the path. The wagon made a chattering noise as it ran over the small bumps in the path leading up to Jean's place.

"Sounds like they're already here. What do you think we should tell them?" Jean asked Steve.

Steve rubbed his chin and thought for a moment.

"I think the less people who know about this, the better. I'm not worried about the kids because they are young and have active imaginations. If they should let it slip, it could be passed off as just a story."

Jean looked worried as she asked, "What are you going to tell them?"

"I know the two of us hate not telling the truth, but in this case, we're going to have to do what it takes to protect the both us. I'll come up with something. Why don't you go meet them?"

Jean went outside to greet Samuel and Abigail. Steve, meanwhile, pondered the upcoming situation. He was going to be put on the spot and had no idea what he was going to say. Nevertheless, that was okay because he was at his best when under pressure. He always had the ability to come up with the right words at the right time unrehearsed.

Abigail was the first to come through the door. She was as he had pictured her—short but shapely. Her tan dress flowed to the floor and was buttoned to the neck. Her brown hair was pulled back and in a bun. Steve could see that Tommy got his looks from his mother.

Samuel followed in behind Jean. She introduced Abigail to Steve.

"Abigail, I would like you to meet Steve. Steve, this is Abigail, and you remember Samuel, don't you?" Jean said, gesturing with her hands toward Samuel.

Steve nodded in the direction of the two.

"Nice to meet you, ma'am."

Steve extended his good arm to shake Samuel's hand.

"And, Samuel, I didn't get to properly thank you the other day for picking me up in your wagon. I was a bit under the weather, but thank you so much."

Steve was surprised at the strong grip of the big man as they shook hands. It almost hurt.

"Well, Mr. Steve, it looks as though you've had quite the nasty fall," Abigail said.

"Yes, it was. That is, what I can remember of it."

Steve was getting into character now. He knew the words would come at the right time.

He continued, "As I remember it, I was tracking a huge bear. I first saw him at the river, and I thought if I could get him, the pelt itself would fetch a good bit of money. I was only about a hundred yards away when he must have gotten a whiff of my scent because he stood on his hind legs, bellowed loudly, turned, and ran. He must have stood a good eight to nine feet tall. I saw him run up into the woods. I ran after him at an angle, hoping to get a shot off. I lost him in the thick brush, but I could hear him forging ahead. After a bit, the sound of the beast bashing his way through the forest stopped. I stood motionless, still hoping to hear something.

"That's when it happened. I was standing in a small clearing, and the snort was the first thing I heard. I turned toward the noise only to come face-to-face with the charging beast. He hit me with such a force, I was knocked out cold. That's all I remember until I woke up staring at a little boy. By the way, did you find my gear?"

"No, it was just you that we found out there," Samuel said.

Steve was in full swing now. He had a great story going on. He had everyone, including Jean, mesmerized with his bear-hunting adventure. He continued.

"Hmmm. He must have carried me off from the spot where he attacked me. I tell you, when he hit me, it was like running full-bore straight into a tree. I'm surprised he didn't finish me off. The bad thing about this whole ordeal is that I can only remember the attack and my name. Isn't that strange? I can't remember where I am from or why I was out there hunting. It is like my memory is lost in the fog. I'm hoping with time to get back where I came from."

There was a silent pause that seemed to last an eternity to Steve. He wondered if they had bought it. Finally, Abigail spoke up.

"Steve . . . you're very fortunate to be alive and to have Jean taking care of you."

"Thank you, Abigail," Steve replied.

"She is a wonderful person, and if anyone can nurse you back to health, she certainly can. I hope you can find your way back home soon."

Turning to Jean, she said, "Jean dear, is there anything you need to help take care of this poor man?"

Jean was looking at Steve when she answered Abigail. She was a bit in awe at the way he sold himself to Samuel and Abigail. She was even wondering if his story was the truth.

With a monotone and halting voice, she said, "Uh . . . uh, no. Thanks anyway. If something should come up, I'll be sure to send word."

Steve was relieved to hear Abigail's comments. He was a bit concerned about Samuel though. The big man said very little. Did he know Steve's story was a cover-up?

Abigail spoke up. "Okay then, Samuel and I have to go. We need to get back to town. I am sure Samuel's work is backing up. Steve, so very nice to meet you."

She placed her arm in Samuel's and turned to go.

"I'll walk you out," Jean said.

Outside, Samuel again repeated his fatherly instructions that he had previously told Jean.

"If you need anything, if you get into trouble, if things just don't seem right, you ring that school bell. Do you hear me?"

Jean smiled and replied, "Yes, *Pa*."

Samuel helped Abigail into the wagon and climbed aboard himself. He paused before taking the reins.

"What's up now?" Jean asked him.

Samuel just grunted. "Oh, nothing. Giddy up there."

He gave a snap of the reins, and the two of them rode off. Jean knew Samuel was not feeling comfortable.

Jean went back inside to talk with Steve.

"Well, I have to say, Steve, I'm not sure which story is true now. That was quite a show. I know Abigail believed it, and I think Samuel did, but I can tell he questioned it."

Steve was resting on the chair, contemplating how well he did with the first test of his new life.

"I hate lying, but I couldn't let them know the truth," he said. "I think it would have created a disaster if I did that."

Jean answered, "I'm just glad it's over for now. I don't mind telling you it was a bit uncomfortable for me also."

"I'm sorry to do that to you," Steve told her.

Jean was going to be making lunch for the boys in a couple of hours. She asked Steve if he was up to walking over to her cabin to join them for lunch.

"I think I could do that," Steve said. "After all, I've been practicing by going to the outhouse."

They both were laughing at Steve's humor as Jean left for her place.

Steve decided to sit on the swinging bench suspended from the rafters on the porch of the schoolhouse. Sitting there, he looked at his surroundings. Although the grass was green, the trees were tall, and the insects buzzed about, the scene seemed different from what he was used to seeing in the year 2012. There was a peaceful serenity. Although he missed home, the lack of modernization was inspiring.

*   *   *

Tommy and Pierce raced to the porch where Steve was resting. Steve had fallen asleep on the porch swing but woke as the boys approached.

"Ms. Jean said lunch will be ready shortly," Tommy said.

"Okay, I'll clean up and hobble on over."

The boys playfully ran back to Jean's cabin.

Steve inched along on his homemade crutches to Jean's cabin, excited to be seeing new scenery after spending so much time at the schoolhouse. The couple of hundred yards to Jean's place was tough going for him, but the effort was worth the reward.

The porch area on Jean's cabin was not much different from the schoolhouse. He climbed the steps gingerly. He had made it thus far, and he didn't want to fall now. He was about to knock on the door when it opened. Tommy was standing there along with Pierce. They had already finished the soup and homemade bread Jean had made and were headed out the door to finish weeding the vegetable garden.

In the background, he heard Jean say, "Come on in."

Steve entered a large room that had a fireplace against the back wall. The kitchen area was to the right where Jean stood putting the final touches on lunch. Jean had decorated the cabin nicely. It was easy to tell that the cabin had a woman's touch. The household goods would have sold for thousands of dollars in the year 2012 because of their antique value, but here they were everyday, common things. The table was set with what looked like her finest dishware. Jean even had fresh-cut flowers on the table.

"This certainly is a surprise, and it looks great!" Steve told Jean.

"I thought it was time you had a nice meal," Jean said. "You've been through a lot, and I figured you could use a little special treatment today."

Steve smiled and sat down.

"Yeah, this bear-hunting business I've been doing has not been kind to my health."

Both laughed as they sat down to eat. Jean enjoyed the quick wit Steve had. She was glad the boys ate quickly and went back to their chores. She was looking forward to hearing more about Steve.

"So tell me, Steve, anyone special in your life?" she asked.

"At one time."

Jean could tell by the tone of his voice that it seemed to have been a significant relationship.

"Care to talk about it?" she questioned.

"Her name was April. I met her while serving in the military. I loved her almost from the moment I met her. I treated her with every good thing I could. I gave her my time. I gave her gifts. I gave her my heart completely. We used to take long walks in the moonlight, talking and loving. I trusted her with everything I had. In the end, she hurt me. We were to marry, but one day, without warning, she left me a letter saying she needed her freedom, and that was it. I never saw her again. It's been a long time. I am not sure I am quite over it yet. So far, no one has come along who could take her place."

Jean could hear the heartbrokenness in his voice.

"I also was hurt once. I was to marry a guy who ended up going back east. Not too long after that, I received a telegram just saying he was sorry and not to expect him to return. Whatever that meant. I could only imagine the worst. Samuel and Abigail helped me a lot to get through the pain."

"I guess it's true," Steve said.

"What's that?"

"Love is forever."

"Love is forever? What do you mean?"

"Times change, but when love hurts, it hurts the same now as it does 150 he could have convinced her to change her mind years from now. The emotion doesn't change from one generation to the next," he said.

Chapter 8

Days turned into weeks. Jean and Steve continued sharing meals together. They spent time sitting on the porch, listening to each other talk. At times, they just sat and listened to the sounds of nature or watched the sunset together.

Each morning, Steve felt further and further from the year of 2012. He wondered if he would ever return to where he came from. His new life had now been going on for over three months. He missed his parents and friends tremendously. He worried about his business. He wondered whatever happened to that silly, mysterious crate he had on board when he crashed. He still could not answer how all this happened. However, he had grown to accept it.

His injuries were healing nicely. He now could walk without using crutches and had full motion of his broken arm. He spent his days doing manual labor for Jean to rebuild his strength. Jean continued to allow him to stay in the room at the back of the schoolhouse.

One evening, the two of them sat together on the porch swing, watching a summertime thunderstorm. The rain was coming down steadily. The sky flashed with electricity. The thunder rolled in gently as if being ushered in on the rain. It was a peaceful setting. No words were being spoken when all of a sudden, a huge lightning bolt struck the school bell. The thunderous clap startled Jean so much, she reactively reached out and wrapped her arms around Steve. She lingered until the thunderous sound rolled off into the valley.

"Uh . . . I'm sorry. That scared me a bit," she apologized to Steve as she pulled herself away.

She was a bit embarrassed by her actions.

"Don't worry about it. I didn't mind," Steve said as he looked into her eyes.

The flashes of lightning illuminated the tenderness in his expressions. Over the last few weeks, Jean had suspected that Steve was growing fond of her, but that didn't upset her. It actually made her feel special. Steve continued to look in her eyes as he drew closer. Finally, the future met the past in a new way as their lips met for the first time. The kiss lingered long after they parted.

*   *   *

That night, Jean cried herself to sleep. She didn't want this to happen. She was afraid of the outcome of that kiss. Deep down, she was fighting her heart. Her inner being wanted the kiss to continue and flourish into romance. However, she was afraid that if she got involved, he would leave her like her former fiancé did. She couldn't face another hurt like that.

Steve was anxious to see her again the next day. It had been a long time since he felt the warmness of the heart and the softness of a woman's lips. It left him feeling pretty excited about life. He knew the consequences that his actions might cause, but he was willing to risk it all.

The next morning, Steve went to Jean's cabin and knocked on the door. There was no answer. He knocked again, but still no answer. He knocked harder on the third time. Finally, Jean called out.

"Please stop. I don't feel like seeing you today. Please just go away."

Steve was crushed with her actions. He hadn't expected this at all.

"Jean, please come talk to me!"

"No, not now."

"Why?"

"I told you I don't want to talk about it now."

"Is this about the kiss?"

"Not really. I just don't want to talk right now. Don't you have some chores to do?" she sternly asked.

"Fine!"

Steve turned and muttered to himself, "Women."

He was trying to convince himself that he was disgusted, but deep down, he was just heartbroken. He went back to clearing brush from around the schoolhouse that he had started doing the day before.

Jean picked up the heart locket that hung from the edge of her mirror. It had been given to her by her former fiancé when the two of them went on a shopping trip for their upcoming wedding. She clasped both hands around it and held it to her chest.

"Why did you do this to me?" she whispered to herself.

Softly she cried over her lost lover.

After sobbing for a few minutes, she remembered what Samuel had told her shortly after her breakup.

He said, "It's your choice to love or not to love. When you choose to love someone and that person rejects you, that doesn't make your love any less real. You just have to find a different person to channel it through because love comes from within yourself. It's a gift you give others, not something you hide within."

Those words were comforting and certainly seemed to make sense. She was doing exactly what he said. She was trying to hang on to love rather than giving love. She dried her tears and went in search of Steve.

Steve saw Jean coming across the clearing toward the school. He kept swinging the machete and chopping at the underbrush at the base of the building. He didn't stop working when she reached him.

"Steve?"

He continued to work, ignoring her request.

"Steve, I'm sorry. Will you please talk to me?"

He stopped swinging, and using his left arm, he wiped the sweat from his brow.

"I'm listening," he said with a cocky voice.

"Last night was hard for me. It was hard because I wanted it to happen, but I was afraid of it happening. I loved the touch of your lips on mine and the feel of your body so close. However, I am scared. I don't want to get hurt again. This morning, it was easier to hide than to face my feelings. I really have grown to like you. Do you understand?"

Steve was still feeling the effects of rejection and lashed out at her.

"It was a simple kiss. What's wrong with that? I wasn't asking you to stay the night with me! I didn't get down on one knee and say 'Marry me,' did I? No, I simply felt a closeness that I haven't felt in a long time, and I acted on it. That's not wrong. We're two people who I thought enjoyed each other's company."

Jean began to cry as she snapped back at him, "I came to apologize, not to be scolded! I didn't say anything about staying the night together or even marriage. I just don't want to be hurt."

She buried her face into her hands and sobbed. Steve sighed and dropped the machete to the ground. He could see he hurt her, and that wasn't what he wanted to do. He was acting selfishly. He pulled her body into his arms and held her close.

Tenderly he said, "I'm sorry. This whole ordeal has been hard on both of us. We both didn't ask to be in this position, but here we are. We both are victims of time and uncertainty."

He allowed her to cry in his arms as he softly stroked her hair.

"Jean, let's agree to take it one day at a time. Does that sound fair? We have built a friendship. Let's not lose that over a kiss. I'm not looking for our friendship to build into a romance, but I won't fight it if it does. I don't want a relationship just for the sake of having a relationship. I want it to be special. Next time, I want it to be the last relationship for me. One that will last a lifetime."

Jean simply answered, "Okay."

"Come on, let's go for a walk and just enjoy each other's company," Steve said.

They walked and talked for some time, and by the end of the day, they were holding hands and feeling a budding romance.

*   *   *

Through the coming weeks, the two of them spent many evenings together snuggled around a blazing fireplace, sipping coffee or hot cider. A romance had developed. The emotions Steve allowed himself to feel reminded him of a time in Hawaii. Jean's nature and appearance was much like that of April's. Nevertheless, although the romance evoked memories of her, he was determined that this was different. Jean's love was new and fresh.

Neither was in a hurry to rush the relationship. They both allowed the friendship to continue to flourish between them first. Besides, Jean still fought the feelings of being hurt because of the experience she had with her departed fiancé.

The rumors in town didn't stop. The single guys who had been rebuffed by Jean in the past were jealous of Steve spending so much time with her. They were being critical of him for staying at her place. The women were appalled that a man was staying so near unsupervised. However, deep down, they too were jealous because Steve was such a gentleman and handsome too. It was the view of most that he should have moved on as soon as he healed somewhat, and in their opinion, he had completed that task.

School had resumed sessions, and during the day, Steve would be outside, doing chores or sitting on the front porch of Jean's cabin and enjoying the scenery. He became a friend to the school children. Although the kids enjoyed Steve's company, it was unsettling to the parents. He never was able to outlive the label as the stranger.

It was early one Friday afternoon when Jean allowed the children to leave school earlier than normal. She was looking forward to cooking an evening meal for Steve, sitting by the fireplace, and maybe playing a game of checkers.

She gathered her things from the schoolhouse and stepped out onto the porch. Steve was approximately fifty feet away, chopping firewood. She paused to watch him.

His broad golden-tanned shoulders glistened from the sweat that covered them. As he brought the ax overhead, the muscles would bulge in his shoulders and arms. She admired his masculinity. As he swung the ax into each piece of wood, his muscles rippled across his body. The sight of such strength sent chills throughout Jean's body.

She wished he would turn, see her watching, and sweep her into his arms. She hadn't allowed anyone to get this close to her emotions for some time. Maybe in a sense, never. However, that didn't matter. It was well worth the wait to have Steve touch her heart like he had.

Finally, she called out to him.

"Hey, you, whatya doing over there?"

He turned, placed the head of his ax on the ground, and leaned on the handle.

He saw her sweet smile and said, "What am I doing? I'm just standing here, looking at the most beautiful schoolteacher I know."

"Why, I'm the *only* schoolteacher you know in these parts, Mr. Steve Mitchell, but I'll take the compliment anyway. You look awful warm, and I let the kids go early. Do you want to go for a swim in the pond?" she asked him.

Steve dropped the ax and walked over to her.

"So you want to swim, do you?"

With a quick sweep of his arm, he had her over his shoulder and headed down the path to the pond behind Jean's cabin. Jean gave a feeble attempt to resist. She was enjoying the attention and the strength in which he picked her up.

Steve was in a playful mood. When he reached the shore with Jean still draped over his shoulder, she thought he would stop, but he just kept walking straight into the pond. The both of them began laughing until Steve stumbled and the two of them fell headfirst into the water. Both surfaced giggling like two children.

They spent the next hour just playing in the pond, having a great time. As far as the two of them were concerned, nobody else existed in the world. Steve gathered her into his arms and gently kissed her repeatedly. Both were touched with the love they felt for one another.

That evening, Jean made a delicious stew dinner. Afterward, they settled down in each other's arms in front of the fireplace. The only audible sound was the occasional hoot of an owl, the cry of a lone wolf, and the crackling of the oak logs in the fireplace. However, deep in the hearts of both was a nonverbal conversation going on loud and clear that said, "I love you."

It was late when Jean told Steve that he better return to his room in the schoolhouse. She knew if he didn't leave now, he would not leave at all.

* * *

Jean and Steve were sitting on the porch, enjoying the Saturday morning stillness. Steve, using a hunting knife, continued carving on a block of wood and shaping it into a replica of his airplane to pass the time. He had worked on the carving for several days. He was finished with it, and it looked like his airplane, but he kept fiddling with it because it soothed him to think of his former life. He wished he could take Jean there.

Steve and Jean talked of their future together. He gave in to his feelings for her completely. It was evident to him that he was locked in this time frame, and he wasn't going to pass up a love like hers. It was so unbelievable, but he was again giving his heart to someone he knew for such a relatively short time.

As the two talked of what could be, Tommy and Pierce could be seen coming down the path.

"Here come your buddies," Jean said to Steve.

The two boys had spent a lot of time with Steve. The two of them enjoyed talking with him. The stories he would tell the boys seemed simple and real to Steve, but because the two boys had never heard of such things like cars, airplanes, and future machinery, it was all so unimaginable to them.

"Hi, boys. What are you guys up to today?" Steve asked.

"We're working for Ms. Crabtree," Tommy said.

"Yeah, she's paying us a nickel for telling as many folks as we can about the barn dance at the Crabtree farm next Friday night," Pierce added.

"Are you and Ms. Jean going to come?" Tommy asked.

Steve smiled at Jean and said, "Yes, I think we will."

Steve and Jean were smiling because they knew the rumors around town about the two of them. They both knew there were plenty of single guys who would be very interested in escorting Jean to the dance. However, she had no interest in them. The jealousy some of the town folk possessed regarding Steve was evident to just about everyone.

Tommy looked at the carving of Steve's airplane.

"Wow, Steve! That sure looks great. Those things actually can fly?" he asked.

"They sure can, and they can fly faster than anything you can imagine."

Steve saw the look in Tommy's eyes. He could see his longing to understand how these things called airplanes actually worked. If Tommy had lived in the twenty-first century, he would have been wingtip to wingtip with Steve, flying some of the most sophisticated planes in the world.

Steve took the hunting knife and carved 1144Q into each side of the wooden fuselage. He held it at a distance, stared at it temporarily, turned to Tommy, and said, "Here, this is for you."

There was a strange exchange of emotions between Tommy and Steve as Tommy reached out and accepted the carving from his hand. Both felt it, but neither spoke of it.

Pierce and Tommy left to finish their job of telling the other neighbors of the dance. With Steve's carving stuck in Tommy's back pocket, he watched the two boys run down the path.

Chapter 9

J acob shuffled up to the bar.

"Give me a whiskey," he told the bartender.

The bartender poured the drink and pointed to Jacob's buddies Leroy and Jack.

"I think they want you over there," he said.

Jacob tossed some coins on the bar and joined his friends at a table in the corner.

Jacob could tell by the mischievous smiles on his friends' faces that they were scheming something, and he wanted in on it. Leroy talked first.

"You know, Jacob, Jack and I were talking how much this Steve guy gets under our skin. Who does this guy think he is to walk into our town and try to take our women? I think we need to do something about it."

"This guy has got to go," Jack added.

"What do you think we should do?" Jacob asked.

Leroy continued, "I think we should go to the dance Friday night, and during the dance, let's get Steve to have a drink with us."

Leroy lifted his head and looked around. He didn't want anyone to hear what he was about to say.

"Then once we get him away from Jean," he continued, "we'll convince him to go night rabbit hunting with us. We'll take him into the woods by the river, kill him, and claim it was an accident."

Leroy now had an even bigger grin on his face.

"You mean, like shoot him dead?" Jacob asked.

"Yeah, that's usually what killing means," Jack said sarcastically. "Remember, we can always say it was an accident."

Shrugging, Leroy added, "Who's not going to believe us?"

Jacob took a huge swig of whiskey, coughed, and said, "You guys are out of your mind. But I love it. I'm in."

The plan was set. All three agreed. Come next Saturday morning, this Steve guy would be out of town for good, and nobody would be the wiser.

* * *

Steve bathed in the pond out back that Friday afternoon before the dance. He was getting ready for a date in town with Jean. This would be the first time they would be seen in public as a couple. He looked through the clothes Samuel had given him back when

Steve first arrived at Jean's place. He was now used to shaving with a true straight-edge razor. The 1860s offered no fancy creams or specially designed razors; they hadn't been invented yet.

Steve picked out a beige shirt and brown pants. He combed his wavy blond hair, and afterward, he stood looking in the mirror. The image he saw of himself was different from what he was accustomed to back in the year 2012. He saw someone different, someone who had adapted to living in the 1860s. Gone were the closely shaved faces, the fancy clothes, and the smooth skin he was so used to having. He now looked like a settler with his wrinkled clothes and weathered skin.

Jean was taking extra time to dress for the evening. She wanted to look her best. She wore a brown skirt with a white blouse. She pulled her auburn-colored hair up into a bun. Months earlier, she had purchased some expensive facial creams from a traveling salesperson. She was saving it for a special occasion, and she determined tonight was the occasion she was waiting for. She was thrilled to be going to the town dance with Steve. She was so proud of him. He was the best thing that had ever happened to her.

Jean heard a knock at the door. It was Steve. He momentarily stood there with the setting sun shining behind him. The sunlight cast a glow around his muscular body. Her heart felt so close to his. He was the most handsome man she had ever seen.

Steve was equally impressed with Jean. He realized that although fancy clothes and makeup were nonexistent, Jean possessed a beauty that didn't need outside help. He could feel his soul connected to hers by a deep love and emotion. He crossed the room, took her hands in his, and softly kissed her neck. He worked his way around to her slightly parted lips. He kissed them gently but passionately and whispered, "I love you, Jean."

She seductively returned his kiss. As she held him closely, she could feel his masculinity envelop her. She trusted him fully and could not imagine life without him. She knew the extraordinary circumstances of how he came into her life, but now that didn't matter. She lived for today, and today he was in her life. Today was special. It was at that moment, she determined she didn't want Steve to leave her arms that night. Tonight would be the night she was going to give herself completely to him. She concluded no man, other than Steve, would ever touch her again.

The two of them walked arm in arm to the horse-drawn wagon Steve had parked in front of her cabin. He helped Jean into the wagon, and the two of them rode off to the dance. This was a dance that both of them had looked forward to.

* * *

About half of the guests were already at the Crabtree farm when Steve and Jean's wagon rolled up. Tommy and Pierce were there with the other children, playing a game of hide-and-seek around the wagons already parked. Steve noticed the carving of the airplane he had given to Tommy stuck in his rear pocket. It made him chuckle at the boyish charm. Tommy was so fascinated with the concept of an airplane.

Steve helped Jean from the wagon.

"Do you feel like all eyes are on us?" she whispered to him as she climbed down.

"Yes, I do, but that's because the most beautiful woman of all has just arrived. Welcome to the royal ball, my queen," Steve said majestically.

Jean smiled and said, "Thank you, Sir Steven."

She playfully stuck her nose in the air and draped her hand for Steve to kiss it as if she were royalty.

The two of them walked arm in arm to where everyone had gathered. It was true; all eyes were on the two of them. Most knew of Steve's amazing bear story and his stay in their township. Some were critical of his story's validity while others believed it to be true because of the injuries he had when he was found. To Steve, he could care less. He had Jean's love, and that was all that mattered.

Samuel and Abigail met them by the refreshment table.

"Well, hi, Steve and Jean," Abigail said brightly.

Weeks earlier, she was a bit hesitant about Steve's intentions, but that had now passed as well as Samuel's suspicions. The four of them chatted while being closely watched by a group of men in the corner. Leroy, Jack, and Jacob were in the middle of that group with drinks in hand, laughing and carrying on.

They hadn't let on to anyone about their plan for Steve that evening. The three of them had made a pact not to discuss it outside their group of three. They wanted no skeletons in the closet. They felt their plan was foolproof.

The music started, and the guests filtered to the dance floor. Those who were not dancing were standing in small groups visiting. The band was made up of local people. The music was not what Steve was accustomed to, and neither was the dancing. Jean and Steve at times laughed almost uncontrollably at his attempt to dance. He was not very good at it in his day, and in the 1860s, he was even worse. The standing joke was if it was not for his two feet, he could dance fairly well. Still, the two of them had a wonderful time.

Steve knew Jean could be someone he could be happy with for the rest of his life. Jean felt the same.

Shortly after the dancing started, Leroy, Jack, and Jacob decided to put their plan into action.

Leroy said to Jack, "Okay, you go and ask for the next dance with Jean. Jacob and I will invite Steve for a drink. After the first dance, look to see if we're still talking with Steve here. If we are, ask Jean for one more dance. If not, meet us at the wagon. It may take us a little time to convince Steve to leave the dance area," Leroy said.

Jack nervously asked, "What if he won't go?"

"Well, if he doesn't, we will force him to go," Leroy answered. "And if he doesn't listen to that, well then, we may have to persuade him further."

Leroy pulled back the edge of his coat to reveal the gun he had strapped to his waist. The three of them smiled and were confident they would be rid of Steve Mitchell for good after tonight.

Steve was dancing close to Jean. They smiled at one another as if no one else was around.

"Jean, do you think—"

He was about to ask Jean if she thought they should get married, but he never had a chance to finish because he felt a tap on his shoulder. He turned to see Jack standing there.

"Jean, may I have this dance?" Jack asked.

Steve started to interrupt and say no when Jean cut him off.

"It's okay, Steve. I've known Jack for some time. Why don't you get something to drink, and I'll be with you as soon as I'm done here."

Steve reluctantly agreed with Jean's graciousness and headed for the refreshments. Steve poured himself a drink. Leroy was standing nearby and asked Steve, "Having a good time?"

"Yes, I am, thanks," Steve answered while keeping his eye on Jean and Jack dancing.

Leroy continued, "That Jean, wow, she's a keeper. She is one beautiful girl, ain't she?"

"Yes, she is," Steve agreed.

He wasn't interested in talking to Leroy. He seemed a little too backwoods for Steve. He just didn't sound like a very bright individual.

Leroy was not going away. He extended his right hand and said, "Leroy is my name. You're Steve Mitchell, right?"

Steve extended his arm and shook hands.

"Pleased to meet you, Leroy, and yes, I am the seemingly famous Steve Mitchell," he said with a bit of displeasure in his voice.

"Ya know, Steve, I've heard a lot about you. I understand you're one adventurous guy. My friend Jacob and I would like to invite you on a little adventure of our own. We like to go rabbit hunting by moonlight, and being there is a full moon tonight, it would be great hunting. These dances always last to the wee hours of the morning, and we thought we would head to the river and get a little hunting in before the party breaks up. We want to invite you along."

"Yeah, it sure is a lot of fun," Jacob added.

Steve was thinking, *What a couple of idiots*, and answered, "No thanks. I don't like rabbit. You guys, I'm sure, will have fun without me."

Steve turned to leave when Leroy grabbed his arm and stopped him.

"Oh, I think you want to go with us."

Leroy pulled back the corner of his coat to reveal the gun strapped to his side.

"Now you just lead the way to the wagons and just keep smiling, or I'll use this thing on you before you get a word out. Do you understand me?" Leroy quietly barked.

Steve was surprised at the turn of events. He looked toward Jean on the dance floor and was trying to catch her eye. However, Jack had already positioned her back to the group, and he was watching the trio's plan unfold over her shoulder. Steve walked toward the wagons, wondering what his next move would be.

When they arrived at the wagons, Jack came running up. When Steve recognized him as the one who was dancing with Jean, it angered him greatly. He looked Leroy in the eye and said, "You leave Jean out of this, or I swear I will hunt you down and kill you with my bare hands!"

"Lighten up, pretty boy. Jean's fine. Now get in the wagon!"

By now, Leroy had his gun shoved in the small of Steve's back.

Steve climbed aboard. Jack and Jacob climbed in the back with him and kept a gun pointed at Steve at all times. Leroy cracked the whip and yelled "Giddy up" to the horses. The wagon lurched forward and headed for the river.

Steve watched the lights of the barn dance grow dim. He wondered about Jean. He never had a chance to say good-bye. Would she wonder if Steve had abandoned her like her fiancé had done? More than that, he never was able to finish asking her about marriage. He had to find a way to get out of this predicament. He was determined that it was not going to end like this. He needed to get back to Jean.

The three thugs shared a bottle of whiskey as the horse-drawn wagon headed for the woods by the river.

"You're going on a rabbit hunt, Mr. Steve Mitchell," Jack teasingly said.

Jacob laughed and added, "And guess who's going to be the rabbit?"

More laughter came from the men.

It was now clear to Steve. If he did not figure something out soon, he would be assured of not seeing Jean ever again. He could not fight his way out. All three guys were fairly big, and besides, they had guns. He had to outsmart them.

"Okay, guys, you got me. I can see where this is heading, but wouldn't you want to make this a little more fun?" Steve asked.

Jack's facial appearance told Steve that he had gotten the attention of at least one of the men.

"What do you mean?" Jack asked slowly.

"Well, you like to hunt rabbits because it's a challenge, right? They're always running back and forth, and that's what makes it fun. So why not let me loose out here and hunt me down? There is a full moon. I certainly can't run like a rabbit, and it's too far to run to town. You are going to kill me anyway. Why not make it challenging? After all, you're the ones with guns, and I'm outnumbered three to one."

Steve could see the wheels turning in the minds of all three of them. He wondered just how stupid these guys were for considering his plan. He wasn't sure if it was their stupidity or the effect of the whiskey that they were drinking.

Leroy brought the wagon to a halt, turned to Steve, and said, "Ya know, Mr. Mitchell, I like the way you think. But just to make sure you don't get away, turn around."

Steve did as he was told, and Leroy took a length of rope and tied his hands behind his back. Steve still was not sure what to do. At least he bought some time and a chance. He knew if he did nothing, he would be executed in cold blood. It was fairly obvious this is what the three men had in mind.

Leroy pulled the rope ends tight around Steve's wrists and told him to get out. Steve scooted to the end of the wagon and dropped to the ground. He stood up and looked at his three captors.

"Well, son, a rabbit doesn't stand still. Now git!" Leroy shouted.

Steve turned and ran into the woods as the three men stood on the wagon and laughed. A couple of shots were fired over Steve's head to scare him.

His heart raced with adrenaline. He had to rely on his memory from his military boot camp days to elude capture and certain death from these thugs. However, in the military, he was never hunted with live ammo. He knew this was his only chance if he was to get out alive.

The branches slapped his face hard as he ran through the woods. With his hands firmly tied behind him, he couldn't fend off the hits. He heard Leroy shout instructions to Jacob and Jack.

"Jack, you take the left. Jacob, go to the right, and I'll go down the middle. He can't get far. The river is just in front of him."

Steve hid beneath a bush, trying to get his bearings, instinctively relying on his military training. The theory of divide and conquer was already accomplished by the three hunters. They split themselves up. Steve rationalized that the river was his best cover. Maybe he could hide underwater to elude this group of madmen.

Steve tried to run as quietly as possible. It made it difficult to have his hands tied behind his back, but he didn't have time to figure out a way to untie them yet. He needed to reach the river in the hope of escaping.

He stopped and listened for the three hunters. It was not hard to tell where they were. They certainly had no concept of sneaking up on the enemy. Jack had even made up a little song about hunting Steve and was singing it aloud. Steve thought his only friend right now was the whiskey the three of them guzzled before all this happened. He could tell by sound that the closest person to him was Leroy coming from behind.

The moonlight helped Steve find his way. The light illuminated the larger objects, but the smaller tree branches were hard to pick up. He could taste blood running down his face from cuts that opened from the brush hitting him in the face. Steve was breathing heavily from all the activity and the adrenaline. He also was thinking of Jean. He had to survive! He needed to see her again. He didn't want to leave her alone.

Through the trees, Steve caught a glimpse of water up ahead. He could see he was getting closer to the river. Soon he was going to have to stop and somehow get rid of the rope that kept him bound. He would need his hands to swim.

Finally, Steve reached the river only to have his heart sink with disappointment. The shore was twenty-five feet above the river. He was on a ridge. He turned to go to the right, hoping to get to the riverbank that way, but he saw Jacob coming through the woods to the right.

"I found him!" Jacob excitedly said as he started firing at Steve.

Steve dropped to the ground. He could hear Leroy coming up from behind, and he could see Jack to the left had already taken aim on his body.

Steve's adrenaline pumped even harder. He was only a trigger pull away from being dead! His hands were still tied behind him, but it was now or never. Steve rolled into a crouched position, jumped up, and ran back toward the cliff towering above the river. He could feel the shot from Jack's gun graze the back of his shirt as he ran. When he reached the cliff that rose far above the water, he dove headfirst over the edge without hesitation. He hoped the water was deep enough, but there wasn't time to scope out a landing area. Certain death waited for him on top.

Time slowed as the murky water came closer to Steve's body as he hurled headlong over the cliff. He could see ripples in the water illuminated by moonlight as they worked their way toward shore. He waited to hit the water . . . he waited to see if he was going to survive this night. Time seemed to be standing still as it had during his plane crash.

Just as he was about to dive beneath the surface, he spotted a black object lurking in the water just below him. It was too late! He couldn't position his body from the collision course he was on. He felt no pain as his head bounced violently off the large tree log floating in the water. Silence overtook him. He no longer felt his hands tied behind his back. He didn't feel the wetness of the water invade his body. He had no concept of his surroundings. As he sank deeper in the water, his silence was soon encased in darkness.

Chapter 10

The heart monitor made a constant drone of a beep. Steve could hear faint movement as though it were a distant sound. Shades of yellows, blues, and greens started to invade the deepest depths of his mind. His senses could detect a new surrounding from where he seemed to be moments before hitting the water. The names Leroy, Jack, and Jacob seemed to float throughout his thought patterns. Things were returning to his memory. He was remembering the river, the hunt, and the jump into the water and Jean. He tried to call her name, but the words just would not form on his lips.

The beeping was now becoming more distinct. Each beep seemed to move him closer to an awareness that moved him further from the reality he thought he knew. He sighed with a small groan.

"Jean . . . Jean," he finally managed to softly whisper.

"Nurse Higgins! Nurse Higgins! He's moving, he's moving! Nurse Higgins—" came the excited voice of Steve's mom.

Nurse Higgins, a rigid German nurse, raced around the corner of the nurse's station to see what all the excitement was about.

"He groaned . . . he moved his head . . . he moved it back and forth, and he whispered the name Jean!"

Steve's mom could barely get the words out; she was so excited. She had spent every day during the last four weeks at Steve's bedside. She just knew in her heart that her son would someday wake from the coma he suffered from the plane crash.

As Nurse Higgins checked various monitors and connections, it was apparent that she too had an element of surprise about the turn of events. She had spent three years in a mobile medical facility deep in the Vietnamese jungle, treating severely wounded soldiers during the early '70s. She had seen aircraft-crash victims, and very rarely did they survive. To see Steve stirring after only four weeks truly was a miracle to her.

Steve could now see vague images. His mind still was as blurry as his eyesight. However, there came a reassuring calm as his mother brushed the hair from his forehead. Without a doubt, he recognized the touch. He knew he was back home. He now could put some closure to an unbelievable dream. However, did he want to? He had built a life in a faraway place, a life that had all the elements of a beautiful love affair—a life that tugged hard at the deepest emotions of his heart.

"Where am I?" Steve managed to get his lips and mouth to speak.

His mom calmly answered, "Honey, you're in St. Luke's Hospital in Saint Paul."

She quickly wiped her tears of joy away. Reluctantly, she released her grip on Steve's hand and raced out the door in search of his father.

As Nurse Higgins checked his vital signs, she explained to Steve what had happened. "You were in a plane crash and hurt pretty bad, honey, and you've been comatose for the last four weeks. You're one lucky son of a gun to be alive," she said in a husky tone. "Your mother is gone to call your dad from the coffee shop. That's become his second home since you've been here."

Nurse Higgins continued to poke and prod Steve to make sure everything was functioning properly.

"It was real touch and go for a while. You were one sorry sight when they brought you into the ER. During the first week, we didn't think you were going to make it. However, you fooled everyone, and here, four weeks later, you're stirring around. I am truly amazed," Nurse Higgins exclaimed.

Richard, Steve's dad, raced into the room with Steve's mom close on his heels.

"Steve, Steve, I . . . I can't . . . I can't believe." Richard was so excited that he could hardly talk.

"Dad, it's okay. The plane was insured," Steve managed to say with a slight smile.

He knew his dad was overwhelmed with emotion. In fact, Steve also was beginning to have a few tears well up from the unprecedented turn of events.

He was torn between the emotion of being back home and the emotion he was still feeling for a person named Jean. Due to the modern technology that surrounded him, it was beginning to sink in that living in the 1800s was only a vivid dream. But was it really? He never had such an experience. He felt pain. He smelled food, flowers, and green grass. He felt love. What he thought was reality for the last couple of months was now gone. *The imagination is a powerful force*, he thought.

No matter how Steve tried to rationalize it, he still couldn't get Jean from his thoughts. He envisioned her innocent beauty. He remembered the long talks while sitting on Jean's porch, watching the sunsets. He remembered the seductive kiss she gave him before the dance. How could that have been a dream? It seemed just moments ago that she was in his arms on the dance floor and he was ready to talk to her about marriage. He thought of her being left alone again. Steve wondered what had happened. He needed closure.

Steve was still thinking of her as he faded into a deep sleep. At 3:00 a.m., Steve was awakened by a touch on his arm. He opened his eyes and immediately was astonished to see a beautiful young woman. She had auburn hair and brown eyes that went well with her smooth complexion. Steve was so awestruck with her because she looked so much like Jean.

He had to ask, "Excuse me, is your name Jean?"

"No, it's Julie," she answered. "And I'm so glad to finally hear you talk. I've been holding a conversation with you nightly, and now you are finally answering me," Julie said. "It's thrilling!"

Steve couldn't believe the resemblance of Julie to Jean. He wondered if his memories of Jean were real or if they were the memories of Julie. She had attended to him nightly, and maybe during his coma, he actually was hearing her and feeling her touch. Somehow in a hallucinating way, he may have transformed Julie's attention into the character of Jean.

"Vitals are looking good, Steve," Julie said. "Maybe soon you can get out of here. Why don't you go back to sleep now. It has been a trying day for you, I am sure." Julie fluffed his pillow, turned, and walked out the door. Steve wondered what was real anymore. One thing was for sure: it was true he had a very trying day.

*   *   *

It had been a week since Steve had awakened from his coma. Prior to that, the doctors had placed a cast on his right arm and leg because of the fractures. He thought about his injuries and how he remembered Jean taking care of them. The injuries the doctors and nurses treated seemed to mirror the injuries he remembered Jean taking care of.

Steve tried to explain to his family and the medical staff the dream he had while in the coma.

Researchers from the University of Minnesota were interested in talking to him once he was on his feet. They wanted to compare his treatment to the events in his dream. It appeared Steve's inner mind was functioning and was well aware of his surroundings. However, the translation of those surroundings was somehow skewed within the inner mind, breaking the communication connection with his ability to reason.

Steve resolved the fact that it was just a dream. The characters he remembered were all a figment of his imagination. Jean, Tommy, Pierce, Samuel, Abigail, Leroy, Jack, Jacob, and of course the rest of the town folk were created by his inner mind. Without the connection to reason it, all seemed real to him. During the last four weeks, Steve's mind could not function outwardly but inwardly. It could not determine fact from fiction. He appeared to have created his own world, a world far from the present day.

The day finally arrived when Steve could leave the hospital. While waiting to be discharged, he talked with his dad.

"So tell me, Dad, is there much left of my plane?"

"Not much. It was pretty scattered and burned. They have it in a hangar at the airport. The NTSB has been going over it to find a cause for the crash," Richard said.

"I had a crate in the back of the plane that I was to deliver to California. Did that survive?" Steve nervously asked.

"Well, kind of. They found the crate. It was scorched but fairly intact. The strange thing is, the lock that held those metal bands in place, well, it was found unlocked. What was in that?"

"Unlocked?" That made Steve curious. It was a strong lock and wouldn't have been easily broken. "It was supposed to have contained a rare African artifact. But now I'm not sure. I'll have to deal with that when I get back on my feet," he answered his dad.

He was somewhat of a celebrity now. The newscasters had followed his story from day one of the crash. A local television news station helicopter was the rescuing aircraft that found the wreckage of Steve's plane after the storm had passed. The plane was totally destroyed, and Steve was lucky to have had the seat belt fail. Without it failing, he would have been trapped in the wreckage and burned to death. Fortunately, he was thrown clear.

Steve felt honored that Julie came to see him off. She was his night nurse for the entire time he was hospitalized. She sacrificed her sleep just to come see him off that morning. As he sat in the wheelchair that would take him to the front doors of the hospital, she leaned down and kissed his cheek.

She whispered in his ear, "Stay in touch with me, okay?"

Steve said he would be glad to.

Steve exited the elevator in the front lobby to a cast of family, friends, and news reporters. Trudy was there. She jokingly told him that by losing a plane, he was cutting hours from her workload of taking care of his stable of planes and that she wanted a raise for it.

Steve's mom and dad were the happiest to see their son leaving the hospital. They had kept a continuing vigil by his bedside, hoping and praying this day would come.

Steve was helped into his parents' car. He waved to the crowd as he left for his parent's home in Albert Lea. It was a ninety-mile journey he had started more than a month ago. As the car pulled from the hospital crowd, Steve kept his eyes on Julie. It was a mystery how much she reminded him of Jean, a mystery he thought would never be solved.

* * *

"Here it is! Great-grandpa's treasure chest!"

Steve's dad was grinning ear to ear as he wheeled the chest into the family room. The day of the opening had finally come. Steve had not seen it for many years, and it sure looked smaller than what he remembered. All the family was present. Aunts, uncles, nieces, and nephews filled the room. Everyone had a curiosity about this chest. Anticipation in everyone was running high.

Richard paused and looked at the chest with admiration.

"Do you know how long I have wanted to open this thing?" he asked those in the room. "Why, when I was a kid, I wanted to secretly take the lock off and look in. But I knew my dad would see the marks on the lock and, boy, would I get it."

Steve called out, "Enough with the speeches, Dad! Open the silly thing, will ya?"

Richard took a chisel and placed it on the lock. With one mighty swing of a hammer, the rusted lock moved but didn't break. It took a couple of powerful hits to finally break it open. Richard carefully threaded the shank of the lock back through the clasp. He momentarily paused before lifting the clasp.

"Well, Great-grandpa Thomas, what do you have in store for us?" he muttered.

Richard carefully raised the lid and looked inside. The musty smell wrinkled his nose as he peered into the relic. On the very top was a note handwritten obviously by Great-grandpa Thomas. It was dated one week before his death. Richard handed the note to Steve to read. Steve read it aloud.

Dear future loved ones,

I have not met any of you, but it is my hope you will continue the dreams contained here within this chest. Many years ago, when I was but a boy, a young man came to be with us. Beaten and broken he was. However, he always helped me dream. He taught me that reality could be anything you want it to be.

It was because of him that I started keeping this chest of what I believed would be someone's treasure in the future. Contained herein are many items I have collected throughout the years. Although the value of each was minimal at the time, I placed them in this chest in the hope that one hundred or so years later, their value would be increased.

You will find many stocks and bonds to some relatively new companies of my time. I encourage each of you to use these treasures to build your own dreams so your descendants of your future will have a legacy that you left behind for them.

Keep confident in what you do, keep dreaming to refresh the mind, and keep your family close at heart.

Love,
Your great-grandfather, Thomas Mitchell

There were many gasps around the room as Richard pulled each item out one by one. There were stocks to current-day automobile manufacturers and electric and steel companies contained in the chest. There were stock certificates to holding companies that now controlled billions of dollars in investments. There were mint-condition gold and silver coins. The treasure in the chest was almost priceless. The stocks alone in today's value were worth millions of dollars. The electricity of excitement filled the air. The entire family was now rich beyond its wildest dreams.

The final item was a yellowed piece of paper wrapped around an object. A special note was attached to it that simply said, "My fame and fortune, which is now your fame and fortune, all started here." Richard carefully removed the paper that wrapped the object.

What was written on the paper made the entire family gasp with disbelief. Steve was especially moved. Because of the inscription, he wondered if he was responsible for the family's new fortune. Was he the one who inspired his great-grandfather? Was he responsible for his family to be involved heavily with the aircraft industry? The turn of events was all so unbelievable.

As Steve held the yellowed piece of paper, his hands trembled almost uncontrollably. It was a crude picture of an airplane. The inscription at the bottom simply said, "To Tommy! Steve Mitchell, May 1863." The object the piece of paper was wrapped around contained a crude wooden carving of a twin-engine plane with 1144Q inscribed on each side.

Steve was awestruck. It wasn't a dream. He actually visited 1863! *But how?* he wondered.

Over the next several days, there certainly were going to be a lot of questions asked. He couldn't answer any of them yet. He thought that his first place to start, though, was going to be that mysterious wooden crate.

The End

Printed in the United States
by Baker & Taylor Publisher Services